CRIME FICTION

CRIME FICTION
*UEA Postgraduate
Creative Writing Anthology
2017*

CONTENTS

DENISE MINA
Foreword

Graham Greene's snobbishness stood greatly in the way of his genius. He called his thrillers 'entertainments' to differentiate them from his more literary works which are often more reflective and internal. Like many of us, he was never without someone to look down on. But he adored crime fiction and thrillers.

His review of *Pépé Le Moko* is a bald paean to the form: it was 'one of the most exciting and moving films I can remember seeing.' He sounds startled in the *Spectator* review, and freshly in love. It's not surprising when you watch *Pépé Le Moko* because it speaks of more than a simple rupture-and-return to social order. It talks about redemption and diamonds, cops and robbers, self-sacrifice and love.

Many of us recognise that moment when we realised that crime fiction, far from just an entertainment, can also be profound. Given the breadth of subject matter, milieu and style in crime fiction, on full display in this anthology, the essential issue is the central place of narrative action in the genre.

Narrative has always been a devalued creature.

The essential problem is this: readers respond to narrative on a profound level. Narrative is profound. It is how human beings make sense of the world. What are most wars but a fight over whose story is best? What is the afterlife but a much better ending? What are corporations and countries but fictional characters?

Churlishness about narrative aside, the essential nature of crime fiction is the hanging question in the reader's mind, the draw of the flume that takes us to uncomfortable places.

Did he do it? Will she die? Is that true?

These hanging questions inhabit our minds between reads. It is what makes us pause in Marks & Spencer, staring vacantly at packets of vacuum-packed ham, while we go for a brief dip in that pool of wondering.

Many readers can recall a crime fiction story they read years ago.

Often that memory is denuded of writer or publication, but the story itself so startled or disturbed them that it stayed with them. It could have sparked some life-changing thought or introduced a new turn in their thinking. It may have taken them to worlds they would have resisted without a narrative draw or the hanging question. The promise of a distracting narrative brings readers to crime fiction with their defences lowered. They are reading for fun.

The 'entertainment' status of crime fiction is a precious, lovely thing. A gun on the cover is the promise of a story whispered in the ear after a heavy dinner, it is an intimate promise of a journey to another world.

Behold then, the Future Whisperers of Stories Profound and Profane in this anthology. Eleven stories that will leave you with a sinking sadness as you approach the end of each one. And leave you, stranded, in the ham department.

HENRY SUTTON

Introduction

This anthology is the result of many years of work and planning. It is born out of UEA's long heritage of teaching creative writing, yet commitment to forward-thinking programmes and platforms. Creative writing at UEA is premised on excellence, experimentation, originality, and freedom from outside commercial pressures. It is also firmly framed within a literary critical context. The dialogue between the creative and critical is paramount. We are readers before writers.

As such, we understand the importance of the crime fiction genre, especially in the long form. We understand how it's centred on purpose and pertinence. How it prioritises engagement and is not afraid to entertain. How it can enlighten and how it can frighten. We also understand that there are no rules that cannot be broken, no parameters that cannot be breached. To paraphrase Chandler: to exceed the limits of a formula without destroying it is the dream of every writer...

Crime fiction has come a long way since the Golden Age. In fact, it was doing wild and determined things during the Golden Age. The crime genre is vast, incorporating endless subgenres and nuances. Originating, arguably, in the 19th century, it came of age in the 20th and now dominates the literary fictional landscape in the 21st. It is the mode for our times, the narrative for a nervous age. Never has the crime novel seemed more important or necessary. Or just right. It is where the novel is today.

Embracing this concept is not only UEA – which pioneered creative writing MAs in prose fiction, poetry, scriptwriting, and biography and creative non-fiction – it is our students. They are driving this story with their enthusiasm, their dedication, their intelligence, their talent. Students are what make our courses. The students, whose work lies within these pages, are not the writers of tomorrow, they are the writers of today. They have embraced the challenge of creating fiction that moves, in every sense. They illustrate just how dynamic the genre is. They write from a position of critical and theoretical strength and resource, yet with an openness and eagerness to explore the new, to challenge.

The thematic and locational range is vast. We travel from London to Hong Kong, Newcastle to Bordeaux, Bristol to Amsterdam, from Surrey to Jersey, Paris to Tel Aviv, not forgetting Essex. We are taken into the minds of the disturbed and the rational, the methodical and determined, the revengeful, judicial and mistrustful. Murder, as Chandler also said, is a serious business. It's handled here with great care and attention, insight and imagination.

It's been an immense privilege to have played a part and watch these writers of formidable promise grow and develop. To watch success hit the first ever UEA MA Crime Fiction cohort even before graduation. Huge congratulations to Harriet, for achieving such a wonderful book deal, but also of course to Caroline, Geoff, Jennifer, Kate, Marie, Merle, Shane, Steve, Trevor and Suzanne, for not just the deals and awards to come, but the work already done, the work beautifully presented here, and for showing us the way forward, for being brave, and focused. What writers. What spirit. Friends for life.

Henry Sutton
Director, Creative Writing MA Crime Fiction

This diverse anthology comprises the latest work from the 2017 cohort of crime fiction writers studying UEA's renowned Creative Writing MA.

HARRIET TYCE

Harriet Tyce grew up in Edinburgh. She read English at Oxford University and practised as a criminal barrister in London for the best part of ten years. She lives in north London with her family. *Blood Orange* will be published by Wildfire in the UK and Grand Central Publishing in the US in January 2019.

Blood Orange

1

The October sky lies grey above me and my wheelie bag's heavy but I wait for the bus and count my blessings. The trial's finished, kicked out at half time after legal argument on the basis of insufficient evidence – always pleasing to get one up on the prosecution. So my client's over the moon. And biggest plus of all, it's Friday. Weekend. Family time. I've been planning for this – I'm doing things differently tonight. One drink, two at the most, then I'm off home. The bus pulls up and I make my way back over the Thames.

Once I arrive at chambers I go straight to the clerks' room and wait for them to notice me amidst the ringing phones and whir of the photocopier. At last Mark looks up.

'Evening, Miss. The solicitor called – they're well pleased you got that robbery kicked out.'

'Thanks, Mark,' I say. 'The ID evidence was crap. I'm glad it's done, though.'

'Good result. Nothing for Monday, but this has come in for you.' He gestures down to a slim pile of papers that's sitting on his desk, tied together with pink tape. It doesn't look very impressive.

'That's great. Thank you. What is it?' I say.

'A murder. And you're leading it,' he says, handing the papers over with a wink. 'Nice one, Miss.'

He walks out of the room before I can reply. I stand holding it, clerks and pupils moving past me in the usual Friday rush. A murder. Leading my first murder. What I've been building up to all my professional life.

'Alison. Alison!' I focus.

'Are you coming for a drink? We're on the way.' Sankar and Robert, both barristers in their thirties, with a collection of pupils behind them. 'We're meeting Patrick at the Dock.'

Their words sink in. 'Patrick? Which Patrick? Bryars?'

'No, Saunders. Eddie's just finished a case with him and they're celebrating. That fraud, it's finally come to an end.'

'Right. I'll just put these away. See you in there.' Clutching my brief, I walk out of the room, keeping my head down. My neck's flushed warm and I don't want anyone to spot the red blotches.

Safely in my room, I shut the door and check my face, lipstick on, flush toned down with powder. Hands too shaky for eyeliner but I brush my hair and reapply scent, no need to carry the stench of the cells with me.

I push the papers to the back of the desk, catching Matilda's eye in the photograph that sits next to the phone. She's smiling, holding onto an ice cream. I touch her face and turn the photograph face down. My breath catches in my throat. I shake it clear and pick up my bag. I'm only going for one. Then I'll go home and put her to bed and hold her hand until she sleeps. I text Carl to let him know I'll be back soon. Like any good mother.

Tonight it's going to go to plan.

—

Our group fills half of the basement of the bar, a dingy place frequented by criminal lawyers and their clerks. As I walk down the stairs Robert waves his glass at me and I sit down next to him.

'Wine?'

'Wine. Definitely. Only one, though. I want to be home early tonight.'

No one comments. Patrick hasn't said hello. He's sitting on the opposite side of the table, engrossed in conversation with one of the pupils – that Alexia – holding a glass of red wine. Distinguished, handsome. I force myself to look away.

'Looking good, Alison. Had a haircut?' Sankar's buoyant. 'Don't you think she's looking good, Robert, Patrick? Patrick?' More emphasis. Patrick doesn't looking up. Robert turns from talking to one of the junior clerks, nods and toasts me with his pint.

'Well done on the murder! Leading it, too. You'll be a QC before you know it – didn't I tell you, after you did so well in the Court of Appeal last year?'

'Let's not get carried away,' I say. 'But thank you. You seem in a good mood yourself?' My voice is cheerful. I don't care if Patrick noticed me coming in or not.

'It's Friday and I'm off to Suffolk for a week. You should try having a holiday some time.'

I smile, nod. Of course we should. A week on the coast with Carl and Matilda. For a moment I imagine the three of us skipping through the waves together like the playful family portraits to be seen in that sort of holiday cottage. Later we'd eat fish and chips on the beach, wrapped up against the October chill blowing off the North Sea before lighting a fire in the wood burning stove in our perfectly appointed house. Then I remember the file squatting on my desk, the difficulties that Carl has in leaving his clients, all so dependent on their psychotherapist. Matilda's school. Not now.

Robert pours more wine into my glass. I drink it. The conversation flows around me, Robert shouting to Sankar to Patrick and back to me again, peaks and troughs of bad jokes and laughter. More wine. Another glass. More barristers join in, waving a pack of cigarettes around the table. We smoke outside, another, no, no, let me buy some more I keep stealing yours and the search for change and the stumble upstairs to buy some from behind the bar and no Marlboro Lights only Camels but for now who cares yes let's have some more wine, and another glass and another and shots of something sticky and dark and the room and the talk and the jokes whirling faster and faster around me.

'I thought you said you were leaving early.' Focusing now. Patrick, right in front of me. He resembles a silvered Clive Owen from some angles. I look for them, tipping my head one way, another.

'Christ, you're pissed.'

I reach out for his hand but he moves sharply away, looking around him. I sit back in my chair, pushing my hair off my face. Everyone's left now.

'Where is everybody?'

'Club. That place Swish. Fancy it?'

'I thought you were talking to Alexia.'

'So you did notice me when you came in. I wondered...'

'You were the one who was ignoring me. You didn't even look up to say hello.' I try, fail to hide my indignation.

'Hey, no need to get stressed. I was giving Alexia some career advice.'

'I bet you bloody were.' Too late now, all the jealousy spilling out. Why does he always do this to me?

—

We walk together to the club. I try to take his arm a couple of times but he pulls away and before we enter the building he pushes me into a dark corner between two office blocks, grasping my jaw for emphasis.

'Keep your hands off me when we go inside.'

'I never put my hands on you.'

'Bollocks, Alison. The last time we ended up in here you were trying to grope me. You made it so obvious. I'm just trying to protect you.'

'Protect yourself, more like. You don't want to be seen with me. I'm too old...' My voice trailed off.

'If you're going to talk like that you should just go home. It's your marriage I'm trying to protect. Your reputation.'

'You want to get off with Alexia, get me out of the way.' Tears leak out of my eyes, any dignity long gone.

'Stop making a scene.' His mouth's close to my ear, the words quiet. 'If you make a scene I will never speak to you again. Now get off me.'

He pushes me away and walks round the corner. I stumble on my heels, putting my hand against the wall to hold myself up. Instead of the rough texture of cement and brick, there's a sticky substance smeared right where I plant my palm. Steady on my feet now, I smell my hand and retch. Shit. Some joker has smeared shit all over the alleyway wall. The smell does more to sober me up than anything Patrick has hissed at me.

Should I take it as a sign to go? Hell no. There's no way I'm going to leave Patrick to his own devices in that nightclub, not with all those hungry young women desperate to make a good impression on one of chambers' most important instructing solicitors. I scrape the worst of the mess onto a clean bit of wall and walked with assurance to Swish, smiling at the doorman. If I wash my hands for long enough I'll get the stink off. No one will ever know.

—

Tequila? Yes, tequila. Another shot. Yes a third. The music thumps. Dancing now with Robert and Sankar, now with the clerks, now showing the pupils how it's done, smiling, joining hands with them and spinning and back to dancing on my own, my arms waving above my head, twenty again and no cares. Another shot, a gin and tonic, head spinning backwards falling through the beat as my hair falls round my face.

Patrick's in here somewhere but I don't care, not looking out for him, certainly have no idea that he's dancing very closely to Alexia with the smile on his face that should just be for me. I can play that game. I walk over to the bar, a wiggle in my stride. Looking good. Dark hair artfully pushed back from my face, fit for nearly forty – the match of any twenty something in that room. Even Alexia. Especially Alexia. Patrick'll see oh he'll be sorry he'll be so sorry he lost this chance messed this one up...

A new song comes on, with a heavier beat, and two men push past me to get onto the dance floor. I sway on my feet then fall, unable to stop the momentum, my phone dropping hard out of my pocket. As I fall I knock into a woman holding a glass of red wine that spills everywhere, all down her yellow dress and onto my shoes. The woman looks at me in revulsion and turns away. My knees are damp in a pool of spilt booze and I try to gather myself a little before standing.

'Get up.'

I look up, down again.

'Leave me alone.'

'Not when you're in this state. Come on.'

Patrick. I want to cry. 'Stop laughing at me.'

'I'm not laughing at you. I just want you to get up and get out of here. That's enough for one night.'

'Why do you want to help me?'

'Someone has to. All the rest of your chambers have found a table and are knocking back prosecco. We can just go.'

'You'll come with me?'

'If you get on with it.' He reaches out his hand and pulls me up. 'Go outside now. I'll meet you there.'

'My phone...' I look around the floor.

'What about it?'

'I dropped it.' I spot it under a table near the edge of the dance floor and retrieve it. The screen's cracked and it's sticky with beer. I wipe it off on my skirt and trail off out of the club.

—

He doesn't touch me as we walk to chambers. We don't talk, don't discuss it. I unlock the door, getting the alarm code right at the third attempt. He follows me into my room, ripping at my clothes without kissing me before pushing me face down onto the desk. I stand back up, look at him.

'We shouldn't be doing this.'

'You say that every time.'

'I mean it.'

'You say that every time too.' He laughs, pulls me close and kisses me. At first I resist but the smell of him, the taste, overtakes me and I stop saying no.

Harder. Faster. My head thumps into the files on the desk as he thrusts into me from behind, pauses for a moment, moves himself. One hand's pulling into my hair and the other's pushing me down onto the desk. Again and again and then the files fall and as they fall they catch the photograph of Matilda and it falls too and the glass smashes and it's too much but I can't stop him and on and on and no don't stop don't stop, stop it hurts, don't stop until a groan and he's done, standing and wiping and straightening.

'We have to stop doing this, Patrick.' I get off the desk and pull up my pants and tights, tugging my skirt neat down to my knees. He's doing his trousers back up, tucking his shirt in. I try to do up my shirt.

'You ripped off a button.'

'I'm sure you can sew it back on.'

'I can't sew it on right now.'

'No one will notice. They'll be asleep when you get home. It's nearly three in the morning.'

I look around the floor, find the button. Push my feet into my shoes, stumble into the desk. The room's spinning, my head foggy again.

'I mean it. This has to stop.' I'm trying not to cry.

'As I said, you always say that.' He doesn't look at me as he pulls his jacket back on.

'I'm finishing this. I can't deal with it anymore.' Now I'm crying in earnest.

He walks over, holds my face between his palms.

'Alison, you're pissed. You're tired. You know you don't want this to stop. Neither do I.'

'This time I mean it.' I back away from him, trying to look emphatic.

'We'll see.' He leans forward and kisses me on the forehead. 'I'm going to go now. We'll speak next week.'

Patrick leaves before I can argue any more. I slump into the chair beside my desk. If only I didn't get so drunk. I wipe the snot and tears away from my face with my jacket sleeve, until my head slumps onto my shoulder in oblivion.

SUZANNE MUSTACICH

Suzanne Mustacich is an American author and journalist living in Bordeaux. She is a Contributing Editor at *Wine Spectator* magazine, with a background in television. Her narrative non-fiction book *Thirsty Dragon* (Henry Holt, Nov. 2015) won two awards and earned excellent reviews. She read Economics and Political Science at Yale.

s.mustacich@gmail.com

Bordeaux
A Mallord & Ricard Novel

MONDAY

1

The car took the turn from the main road faster than was advisable in the murky pre-dawn darkness, but even so, Captain Max Ricard, a detective in the *Brigade Criminelle*, pressed his hand into the dash, willing the car to go faster. He fervently wished to toss his driver, Lieutenant Sophie Brunel, from the car and drive himself. He glanced at her, the lights from the dashboard illuminating the sweat beaded on her forehead and her white-knuckled grip on the wheel. No flashing lights, no sirens.

'Anytime you want to get us there,' he said.

He felt a satisfying surge of speed as she added pressure to the accelerator. The car hurtled down the narrow road to the Gironde estuary, the headlights showed vineyards radiating in every direction. A grey veil of fog hung over the landscape. Dawn had begun to break. He could barely make out where the fog ended and the limestone walls of a sprawling nineteenth-century chateau began.

'We're sure this road leads to the port?' she asked.

'I know that *jalle* does.' Or he hoped it did. There wasn't a road sign, but along the right side of the road ran a straight, narrow channel of water bordered by high grass. The channel was what the locals called a *jalle*, and it drained the unwanted ground water from the vineyards into the estuary.

'You see the car?' he asked. At 90 km/h, they would crash through the small, battered Citroën parked across the road in approximately 20 seconds. Not that he was worried.

'Tell them to get the hell out of my way. Sir.'

Ricard was already barking orders into the radio handset, and the Citroën, driven by gendarmes from Pauillac, swiftly reversed onto a dirt track wide enough for a tractor needing access to the vineyards.

'No one comes or goes but us,' he said into the handset as they flew past the Citroën.

The Citroën flashed its lights in acknowledgment. They had called to confirm they were in position seven minutes after receiving Ricard's urgent order to set up a roadblock. But the weather combined with the darkness and the many dirt roads traversing the vineyards meant that it was impossible to block every escape route.

'Damn easy for someone to disappear in this fog,' he commented. Even the road disappeared a kilometre ahead of them.

An hour ago, thieves had broken into a warehouse on the outskirts of Bordeaux and stolen wine. Thirty minutes later, a fisherman called in a tip, reporting an unusual degree of activity around an abandoned customs house next to the estuary, ten kilometres north of the break in location. Then they set a van on fire. The torched van matched the modus operandi of a crime ring Ricard had in his sights. The desk sergeant called Ricard immediately, pulling him out of an uneasy sleep.

A memory teased him, then the small car hit a dip in the road and took air. The tyres thudded back to asphalt. His head, already nearly touching the roof, smashed into the hard surface. The right back wheel slid onto the narrow gravel shoulder. Brunel jerked the steering wheel to the left, then sharply right as she turned into the skid, narrowly keeping them out of the channel of water.

'Sorry, sir,' Brunel said automatically.

'Just drive,' he snapped, annoyed all over again that Brunel's Renault hatchback, which barely fitted his long frame, had been operational, while his Audi sat at the body shop for a busted side mirror.

The vineyards gave way to the *palus*, a swathe of fields too soggy for growing grapes. Cows grazed on the tall grass. The road sloped towards the water until it ended at the tiny port of Beychevelle.

Ricard hoisted his body out of the cramped car with the speed of a man half his size and age. He slid his Sig Sauer from its holster. He didn't need to look to know that Brunel shadowed him.

The small parking lot also served as a picnic area, its attractiveness marred by the smell of chemical smoke and the charred remains of a delivery van. Ricard placed his hand gingerly on the metal. Still warm. He allowed himself a small smile when Brunel also touched a finger to the blackened carcass. She often mimicked his actions as if to absorb his instincts.

The only building was a former customs house abandoned decades ago. The windows had been bricked shut. He scanned the surrounding shrubbery. He didn't see anyone as he approached the building. He slowly twisted the door knob. It was locked. Had the thieves unloaded the stolen wine and left? Was someone holed up inside? His ears strained to distinguish between the natural sounds of the estuary and the furtive movements of a fugitive. But it was the distant whine of an engine travelling at a high speed that caused his muscles to tense. His eyes locked on the road. In the distance, a spot of dark blue appeared through the fog, gradually taking a familiar shape as it raced towards them.

Tension was replaced by mild annoyance as he waited impatiently during the three minutes it took for the military van to park, an elite team of heavily-armed gendarmes in blue uniforms, flak jackets, and masks pouring from the back of the van. Despite the balaclava, Ricard recognised their plain-clothes leader immediately.

Ricard met the sergeant, a thick-necked Basque named Josu Eneko with a side-arm strapped to his thigh, in the middle of the parking lot.

Ricard's voice was low. 'Sergeant.'

'Captain.'

The Paulliac gendarmes had clearly alerted the colonel in Bordeaux, setting Eneko and his team in motion.

'See anyone?' asked Eneko.

'No.' Ricard didn't bother to elaborate.

Eneko took in the surrounding fog. 'Not that we would see them,' he grumbled softly. The gendarme's eyes were as hard and black as onyx as they sized up the customs house.

'Locked,' muttered Ricard.

'Allow my team to be of assistance.'

Ricard inclined his head in assent. Following Eneko's silent signal, two gendarmes secured the perimeter of the parking lot while the rest surrounded the customs house. On their leader's nod, a gendarme smashed in the door with a battering ram. An instant later they were inside. Adrenaline junkies all of them, thought Ricard.

Moments later, Eneko came out, caught Ricard's eye. He pulled down his black mask, shook his head, banked fury written on his broad, swarthy face. Ricard didn't have to ask. The building where they'd thought to find at least some of the stolen wine was empty.

'OK, let's seal this off. Search inside, search the perimeter, careful where you walk,' Ricard's deep voice carried.

Gendarmes or not, it was his crime scene. He wanted forensic technicians from the *Police Technique et Scientifique* unit within the *Police Nationale* not the *Gendarmerie*. He turned to Brunel. 'Get crime scene in here.'

'They're on their way,' said Brunel. 'Another technician is already at the warehouse.'

'Good job.'

The grand cru crooks – as Ricard had come to think of them – were skilled at their chosen profession. The PTS forensics specialists had yet to find a trace of saliva, fingerprints, hair or anything else that might unlock their identity. After the second heist, the dossier had landed on Ricard's desk. This was the fifth hit by what was looking increasingly like the same gang of crooks. To complicate matters, the crooks had targeted both urban and rural warehouses, putting the police and gendarmes in competition – not for the first time. Eneko was an *adjudant* or sergeant in the Gendarmerie's *Section de Recherches*, and two similar wine heists had occurred in his rural patch.

Eneko strode over to Ricard. Eneko rolled his shoulders and cracked his neck. The man was built like a bull.

'I really want to get these bastards, Ricard.'

'We will. At least it's only wine, Eneko.' Not child prostitution like the last case they'd worked together.

'Not the kind of wine I can afford to drink,' Eneko snorted.

'You think we're after the same crooks.'

It wasn't a question. Eneko would not have raced to Beychevelle at the crack of dawn unless he had reason.

'Don't you?' asked Eneko.

'It's not unusual to steal a vehicle used in a burglary, then burn it to erase evidence.'

'No, it's not.'

He wondered if the sergeant had information that wasn't contained in the case files. Probably. Ricard worked under the *Directeur Interrégional de la Police Judiciaire* known as the DIPJ, but both he and Eneko answered to the examining magistrate under France's inquisitorial judicial system. It would be a tussle for control of the investigation.

'This is my investigation, Eneko. The warehouse is within our jurisdiction.'

Eneko glanced at their surroundings and then back at Ricard. His meaning was clear. The gendarmes patrolled the French countryside, limiting the jurisdiction of *La Police Nationale* to urban areas.

'If you say so,' conceded Eneko, which made Ricard suspicious. It wasn't like the sergeant to cede terrain to the *Police Nationale*.

Eneko turned away, and his raised voice echoed off the water. 'Stay alert, we might just get lucky, maybe some bastard was sloppy.'

Two crime scene technicians had arrived, donned disposable coveralls and taped off the perimeter around the customs house and the van. They were bagging any scrap they found in the general area: a forgotten can, a dropped cigarette, a scrap of packing tape, anything on which the criminals' DNA might have hitched a ride.

Ricard said to Brunel, 'See if they traced the call that came in.'

She took out her iPhone.

Ricard turned his back on the activity and prowled towards the river. A badly damaged boat slip disappeared into the muddy water, but the narrow 19th-century jetty still held strong. The stones were slick with algae. He strode to the end and took in his surroundings.

He couldn't see much. A thick layer of fog had settled in over the water. Every few seconds the fog shifted and he could just make out the low-lying islands in the middle of the estuary. Moments later they were hidden again.

The islands had once been inhabited, used as pasture and farm land. The islands flooded during the winter storms and the shifting shoals made navigation to and from the islands treacherous. It had been a miserable life. The lone school had closed in the 1970s, and the last of the island communities had left. The buildings still stood, silent and forlorn.

Not a single boat on the river. A hundred years ago, this place would have been busy with water traffic, flat-bottomed boats called *gabarres*, their holds filled with onions and fruit, fish and oysters, shoes and curios, pottery and tiles, hay and lumber, coal and quarried stone, sailing from port to port and back to Bordeaux again. But even then the main lubricant for commerce – and the only excuse for society in this stretch of former swamp – was wine.

There would have been a reason to bring wine here. Wagons would have brought it down from the chateau to the port by the barrel, rolled it onto the gabarre and sailed it to Bordeaux. Even contraband would have left from the port.

These days there weren't many boats, and only one narrow road in and out. With so little traffic, even with the fog, a local might have heard or noticed a car. Would have been easier to pull off on a fire road deep in the forest, unload the wine, torch the van and split.

It just didn't make sense. Why offload the stolen wine here?

He didn't doubt the thieves had been here. The torched van was proof.

These thieves were smart enough not to leave DNA, so why take the risk? Why choose this spot if not to use the abandoned customs house? He flipped the questions back and forth in his mind, but didn't come up with any answers.

Ricard turned at Brunel's footsteps. As she came closer, he noticed that her cat-shaped eyes had the intense look they got when she locked onto a case. If villains stopped behaving badly, the lieutenant would be one bored woman, he thought.

'It was a mobile phone, a pre-paid burner, the kind sold by the post office,' she said.

'So was it a legit tip-off or are they just fucking with us?' he asked.

'Why would they fuck with us?'

Ricard didn't answer. His eyes shifted along the reeds growing along the riverbank, and the trees and the fog, searching for any tell-tale movement. Someone was watching them. He could feel it. The fisherman?

A van pulled in. The crime scene technicians had arrived.

'Keep an eye on them,' he said.

The wind had picked up, but from here he could get a good look at the crime scene. And whoever was watching could get a good look at him.

He glanced north, the direction the estuary flowed until it reached the Atlantic Ocean. Then he walked south, along a narrow path beaten into the river grass, the only access for the fishermen to reach the line of quaint but flimsy wooden fishing shacks on stilts – locals called them *carrelets*, perched above the reeds. The tip had come from a man who said he had fallen asleep in a *carrelet*, and woken to the smell of the van burning.

He reached the first fishing shack, pushed open the small gate and stepped onto the precarious wooden planks that served as an elevated walkway over the reeds and muddy water to the hut. He pushed the door open. There was no wall on the side of the shack facing the water. He walked to the edge where a square net attached to a winch hung suspended from the shack. A sharp wind chilled his face. He smelled the brine of the Atlantic thirty kilometres to the northwest. It would have been a wet, cold place to sleep when there were four walls and a roof at home.

He left the shack. From the plank footbridge he could see part of the parking lot but not the entrance to the customs house. He couldn't see the burned-out van. He craned his head, leaning, and one of the half-rotten planks shifted and he lost his footing. He caught the thin rail as his foot went through the wood up to his thigh and he felt his knee pop.

Painfully, he pulled his leg clear, his heart thumping. The leg stung where the wood had scraped off a few layers of skin. His knee was going to swell like a melon.

That's when he noticed the long black tendrils entwined in the reeds below.

He shouted for Brunel and Eneko, and then he was across the plank walkway, near dragging his damn leg, on the bank and wading into the reeds. He barely registered the shock of cold water seeping into his shoes, clothes and broken skin.

The current was moving swiftly, but the body was caught face up in shallow water by the reeds and branches. It was a young woman and she wore a miniskirt and thigh-high boots. Her eyes were closed. He heard footsteps and voices as his mind registered that the body hadn't yet bloated with gas. He didn't need the medical examiner to tell him it was probably homicide. The woman's coat had slid off her slim shoulders. The bruises around her neck were deep blue. She'd been throttled while she was still alive by someone with large hands. Habit had him leaning over her, his fingers pressing against the carotid artery. You never knew. She wasn't as cold to the touch as he'd expected.

Jesus.

Then he was plunging his arms into the water, lifting the slight body in his arms as he hobbled to shore, cursing his leg.

'Ambulance!' he yelled, laying her down on the grassy bank, yanking his jacket off and wrapping it around her.

'She's alive!'

His voice echoed across the river, then was swallowed by the fog.

2

Ricard fed coins into the coffee machine in the hospital waiting room. His shoes and trousers were still wet and he'd already bought tea and broth from the machine in an attempt to chase the chill from his body. The coffee tasted as bad as he'd expected.

His iPhone rang. It was his mechanic. The side mirror was fixed. 'You have somebody who can drop it off at headquarters?'

Two minutes later, he hung up, relieved to know the Audi was on its way.

Brunel walked in, handed him a small duffel as she ended her call.

'No match with any recent missing persons,' she told him. 'Did you get them to clean up your leg?'

From her coat pocket, she pulled out a small bag of Ricola herbal cough drops, popped one in her mouth and handed him one, even though he hadn't asked. He took it. Thirteen organic herbs grown in the Swiss Alps might just kill the taste of stale coffee in his mouth.

'Not a single Asian woman missing in all of France?'

'Wrong age group. Just a hooker in Lille, a user.'

Ricard agreed with the unspoken conclusion. Their victim didn't have any needle marks. The doctors put her in her early twenties.

'Might not have anything to do with the burglary. Tide was running towards the ocean,' said Ricard. 'She could have gone in upriver.'

'Couldn't have been in there long.'

Rain had swollen the estuary and the currents were fierce. Her unconscious body would have travelled fast.

'Whoever dumped her couldn't have been far away,' said Ricard. Might even have been watching us, he thought. Then they'd know she'd survived.

'She might need security. Make sure no one goes in except medical staff.'

'The super won't OK overtime,' said Brunel.

Not for a half-dead, unknown Asian woman was the unspoken thought. Not when they were already stretched thin. He sighed, stretched his neck to loosen the knots of muscles clamping the base of his skull like a claw. He widened his stance – and his shoes squished.

'I've got to get out of these clothes.'

Ricard went to the men's room, and dabbed the blood from his leg with toilet paper. He quickly changed into dry clothes, and crammed his wet garments into the duffel bag. Thankfully his wallet and phone had stayed dry.

When he came out, a doctor was talking to Brunel. Ricard glanced from the doctor to Brunel and back. The young lieutenant was blushing.

'Captain,' nodded the doctor. 'She's in a coma, hypothermia, severe bruising around her neck. She should be dead.'

'But she's not. Any sign of sexual assault?'

The doctor shook his head.

'We'll do a scan for brain activity, but I'm not hopeful. Her clothes, everything on her was bagged and given to forensics as you asked.'

'Anything else?'

'She has a tattoo around her right ankle. A scorpion and two words in Chinese.'

'You're sure?'

'My intern is Chinese.'

'What does it say?'

'Five and nine.'

'Five and nine? The numbers?'

'The words in Mandarin for the numbers.'

'We'll need a photo of the tattoo. Send it to my email.'

Ricard handed the doctor his business card. He was certain the doctor would have preferred the lieutenant's card. He could have told the doctor he was wasting his time.

'Thanks, doc.'

Ricard and Brunel walked outside.

'She could be our first witness,' said Brunel.

'Our only witness.'

They looked at each other over the roof of Brunel's car.

'We haven't been to the warehouse yet. Crime scene number one,' she said.

He opened the passenger side door, and sandwiched his body into the car.

'We don't know number one, Brunel. Number one is where this whole fucking thing started.'

As he was fastening his seat belt, his phone pinged. He opened the email and stared at the photo of the girl's tattoo. A cold ball of dread settled in his gut. He'd seen tattoos like that before when he worked organised crime in Paris. They had been much more elaborate, but the design had been the same. Every one of them had decorated the body of a Triad member. He suddenly wanted to hear that recording.

'Change of plan. Back to the Commissariat.'

—

'What is your name, sir?' The female officer's voice rang clear and unhurried on the recording.

'Never mind my name. Don't want no trouble, just doing my civic bit,' responded the male caller. Not a local accent, thought Ricard. Marseille maybe.

He leaned back in the plastic chair, his eyes closed as he listened.

'Where are you calling from?'

'I told you. The port of Beychevelle, just south of St Julien.'

'And what did you see exactly?'

'For Christ's sake, I told you, there were guys carrying wood boxes, like they pack wine in, you know what I'm saying?'

'You're sure it was wine?'

'How would I know? Not like I got up and close. But it looked like those wood boxes they use for fancy wine.'

'A wine box?'

'Not the kind you put in the fridge with the spigot.'

'Right. A wood wine box.'

'It was the van burning, woke me up.'

'Woke you up, sir?'

'Yeah, woke me up, *putain*, I'm a fisherman. I was sleeping in the fucking *carrelet*. Listen that's all I got to tell you, but seems like you might want to let *someone* know.'

The call ended abruptly when the man hung up.

Ricard hit play again and listened.

The caller's voice stirred a memory deep in Ricard. Victim? Villain? Witness? He'd met many of all three in nearly twenty years on the force, mainly working out of 36, quai des Orfèvres. Usually a distinctive characteristic stuck with him, like a stain that couldn't be scrubbed clean.

Brunel opened the door, and walked in, handed him a piece of paper.

'What's this?'

'PTS sent it over. It's a photocopy of a business card they found in the pocket of her skirt.'

He nodded, pleased. He'd come to appreciate the efficiency of the provincial city's *Police Technique et Scientifique* unit. They didn't have the resources of the national lab in Écully, but they were meticulous.

'*A. Mallord, Mallord et Fils, négociant en vins,*' he read. A wine merchant. No shortage of wine merchants in Bordeaux.

'You think she's connected to the wine trade?' asked Brunel. She was already Googling the négociant's name on her phone.

'Could be. Could be she's a student, tourist, prostitute, all of the above or none of the above,' he mused. 'A lot of trade between China and Bordeaux.' Not all of it legal.

He studied the photo of the girl's tattoo again.

A decade ago, he had worked a drug operation tied to the production of heroin and synthetic drugs coming out of China. A hundred and fifty years ago the French had hoped to sell wine to China's opium users, providing them with an additional source of intoxication. He didn't think drug addicts in the new China were buying Bordeaux, but nor did they rely on Indian or Afghani heroin. They had a homemade supply now, and the Triads controlled it and exported it.

'Augustus Mallord?' said Brunel, reading the search results. She looked at him. 'There's a funeral today.'

'He's dead?' he asked.

'Not him, his wife. Charlotte Mallord.'

'Address?'

'Rue Notre Dame, the Protestant church in the Chartrons, already started.'

Ricard was on his feet.

'Are we really going to interview him at his wife's funeral?' she asked.

'I am.'

He held up his car keys.

'Got my car back. You're going to lean on PTS. They're backlogged, they're working their asses off, convince them our case is a priority.'

—

Ricard parked the Audi on a yellow line on Cours Xavier Arnozan and walked the two blocks down Rue Notre Dame. It had started to drizzle and the cobblestones glistened where the drops fell.

Rue Notre Dame was a narrow street behind the old wine warehouses that fronted the quay. When he'd been a boy, it was a seedy area with rough bars, abandoned buildings and hookers working in the alleys. For most of its history, the district had been an enclave for people living outside the old city walls. Carthusian monks had taken refuge from the Hundred Years War, gratefully camping in a swamp rather than face genocide in the Dordogne. In the 20 years he'd been away from Bordeaux, the neighbourhood had gone considerably upmarket. He wondered what the Carthusian monks would make of the antique dealers and boho restaurants. After the monks, foreign wine merchants had arrived. And they were still here. He could hear the bagpiper.

The aching melody gnawed at his heart. It was a Scottish hymn that Ricard recognised from his years singing in the boys' choir. He hadn't cared much for choir, but he'd earned extra food by performing at weddings and funerals. He'd sung at funerals like this, for people like this. Then he'd learned to box. His knuckles flexed automatically.

The Temple de Chartrons sat back from the street at 10 rue Notre Dame. The church was tall, but not particularly wide – not nearly large enough to hold the crowd who had come to mourn Charlotte Mallord. A sea of tweed in muted greens, blues and browns bunched near the open doors.

Ricard eyed the austere, neoclassical building. Four Ionic columns supported a triangular pediment. The only decoration was a bas-relief of an open Bible and some clouds. The Protestant wine merchants had wanted to give the impression of power and nobility. They had succeeded.

As he approached the entrance to the church he could hear the singing, couldn't help joining in, his baritone low and rough.

Abide with me, fast falls the eventide,
The darkness deepens, Lord with me abide.
When other helpers fail and comforts flee,
Help of the helpless, O abide with me.

He passed the bagpiper and shouldered his way inside, ignoring the startled looks, keeping to the side of the nave as he walked towards the front of the church, still singing softly. Luckily he was wearing a dark blazer, but the jeans were out of place. A closed casket rested on a table before the altar. Ricard made his way to the last of the great columns, slightly ahead of the front pew, leaned a shoulder against the stone and positioned himself to watch the faces of the mourners as they slowly filed towards the casket draped in a white pall.

Familiar, condescending, patient, free.
Come not to sojourn, but abide with me

Ricard noticed that their eyes drifted inevitably to a proud, elderly man standing in the front pew. His suit was tailored from fine grey wool. He had a head of thick white hair and a straight spine. Augustus Mallord, thought Ricard. Next to Mallord was a man a generation younger, not quite so tall, not quite so striking. Other people, likely family members, filled the rest of the front row seats.

I fear no foe, with Thee at hand to bless;
Ills have no weight, and tears no bitterness.
Where is death's sting? Where, grave, thy victory?
I triumph still, if Thou abide with me.

Ricard studied the older man. He was withdrawn, impassive, ignoring the polite bows of respect offered by the mourners. Grief or boredom? It wasn't clear. Ricard settled in to wait. After several minutes, he sensed a fresh alertness in the man. Mallord saw a woman walking towards the casket. The old man's eyes hooked on her as if drawn by a steel wire.

Ricard shifted his attention to the woman. Her expression was tight. The blonde hair was pulled back in a loose knot. She was nearly as tall as Mallord and had the same lean, strong build. *Valkyrie*, thought Ricard. The fanciful image came to mind and he couldn't shake it. He'd read books about Vikings when he was a teenager. One of the few kids at school on the weekends, there hadn't been much to do so he'd read his way through the library. The Valkyries decided who died in battle, and of the dead, chose the fiercest, most heroic warriors to go to Valhalla, the afterlife ruled by Odin. Ricard had long since given up hope that there was a place for him in an afterlife, but there was no question this woman was prepared for battle.

3

Only death could have brought me to Bordeaux, thought Theodora 'Teddy' Mallord as she stopped in front of the casket. She had seen her grandmother's face for the last time in the narthex of the church, just before the lid shut and the pastor draped a pall over the casket. Glancing up, her eyes met the gaze of the pastor. He stood at the altar, his hands clasped before him, his brow lowered as he squinted at her. He hadn't recognised her in the narthex and couldn't place her now.

Little girls grow up. They travel to dangerous places and return home unrecognisable. They learn to say goodbye to the people they love. It had been fifteen years since she'd last set foot in this church. Then too, it had been with her grandmother. She looked at the casket, and swallowed past the tightness in her chest.

Charlotte Neville Mallord had always seemed more stoic than courageous. Born the sole heir of a Bordeaux wine merchant, who in turn had been the third and only surviving son of an affluent Edinburgh wine merchant and his aristocratic wife, his brothers having died side by side in 1917 in a sodden trench along the Chemin-des-Dames on the Western Front, Charlotte had always known the weight of legacy.

Teddy wanted to linger, sit down on the cold marble floor next to her grandmother's body. Her grief was a solitary beast, uneasy in a crowd. A thin film of sweat had formed on her forehead. The last twenty-four hours hadn't left her with a moment to think. Time seemed to have sped up an instant after it had ground to a halt for her grandmother.

Turning from the casket, she ignored her grandfather's stare. It wasn't difficult. She found it harder to look past the man standing to the right of him, leaning against a column. His dark blazer was off-the-rack and there was nothing casual about him. His gaze was cold and flat. She knew with certainty that he was the police.

GEOFF SMITH

Geoff Smith is an award-winning advertising copywriter and creative director. He was the recipient of the first David Higham Scholarship for Crime Fiction at UEA. He lives in South London with his family and is currently working on the follow-up to *Burner*.

geoffsmith.writer@gmail.com

Burner

Irina ignored the tiny insects that attacked every centimetre of her exposed skin and crawled into her ears and nose. She had endured much worse. Instead she focused her attention on the small, white-painted cottage sitting alone on a grassy promontory fifty metres away in the shadow of the mountains beyond. She could see the occupants through the binoculars. A man and a woman sat next to the small window enjoying their evening meal.

Though it was already ten o'clock, the sky was still light and at this latitude, at this time of year, it would remain so for perhaps another hour. She handed the binoculars back to the man who crouched next to her in the damp grass. He took them with one hand while his other continued to scratch at the insects that were enjoying an evening meal of their own.

'Fucking mozzies.' It was a London accent, working class. She had met Danny Marshall for the first time the day before when he picked her up at Glasgow Airport but she was already becoming tired of his constant whining. Marshall, the car and equipment had all been arranged via her usual dark web recruitment site. She made a mental note not to use him again after this job. But people with his skills weren't always easy to find. Especially in the UK.

'They call them midges here,' said Irina. 'And it is lucky they are out tonight.'

Marshall shot her a quizzical look as he slapped at the back of his thick neck and rubbed another wave of midges into a smear of black pulp and red blood. His blood.

'It means everyone else will stay indoors.'

Irina stood up and checked the mechanism of the Glock 19 Marshall had provided for her. She then tucked it into the waistband of her jeans and pulled her pale blue hiking jacket over to hide the bulge.

'Remember, there must be no shooting,' she said as Marshall got to his feet and checked his own gun. 'These are just to scare them.'

They walked hand in hand up the slight incline towards the house. This had been Irina's idea. They were playing the part of a couple, tired and hungry after a long day's hike, coming to ask directions. If the targets looked out of the window, that's exactly what they would see. She liked every detail to be correct. They stopped at the door and Irina knocked. It was a friendly, rhythmic knock. One tap followed by three fast ones.

A few seconds later a tall, slim, middle-aged man with a mess of curly brown hair and steel-rimmed glasses opened the door. His wife stood just behind him. She was of a similar age but the years had not been so kind to her. Neither of their faces showed fear. Just surprise that anyone should come calling at this late hour.

Irina beamed at them and the couple visibly relaxed a notch.

Then Marshall exploded forwards, slamming his full weight against the door with his shoulder and powering the other man backwards into his wife. The couple lost their balance and fell to the tiled floor.

The woman screamed.

Irina and Marshall stepped into the house and closed the door. Irina levelled her gun at the woman and she stopped screaming. It was a common response, something she had seen time and again whenever she showed a gun to people who were not expecting to see one.

'We are over a kilometre from the nearest neighbour,' said Irina. 'You may scream but I would prefer that you remained quiet. I need to talk to your husband.' She held out her left hand and helped the woman to her feet then motioned for her to sit on the sofa. 'Thank you for your co-operation, Mrs Hicks. Or would you prefer Fiona?'

Fiona Hicks said nothing. Her eyes were wide with fear, her breaths coming in short snatches like a child recovering from a tantrum.

Irina turned towards Hicks as Marshall pulled him to his feet, the gun pressed firmly into the side of his head.

'Dr Hicks,' said Irina, 'please take a seat next to Fiona. I would like to ask you a few questions.'

Hicks did as he was told, his hand slipping into his wife's and squeezing it protectively. Marshall stood to one side covering them both with his gun. Irina took one of the dining chairs and sat down facing the Hickses, resting the gun on her knees.

'We are trying to locate a friend of yours,' said Irina. 'Her name is

Amanda Sawyer.'

Hicks's face reddened and when he spoke his voice sounded stilted, uncertain. 'Amanda? Yes, she is a colleague of mine at the Helix Institute. She left unexpectedly last—'

Irina leant forwards and backhanded Hicks across the face. The impact dislodged Hicks's glasses and a thin trickle of blood started flowing from his bottom lip. He wiped it away with a trembling hand, his face ashen.

'You may lie to your wife but please do not lie to me,' said Irina.

'Steven?' asked Fiona, her voice barely above a whisper. 'What's this about?'

'I am afraid that your husband has been somewhat relaxed in his interpretation of his marriage vows.'

'What the fuck is going on? Who are you?' Hicks began to get up but stopped when Irina raised her gun.

'She is no longer at her flat,' continued Irina. 'And hasn't been at work for several days. We'd like to know where she went.'

'I don't know,' said Hicks. 'She called it off between us a few weeks ago. I assume she has just taken some time off.'

Irina sighed heavily and shook her head. She pushed herself up and crossed to the window where the light from the setting sun was slanting in, casting long shadows. She took a deep breath before turning back. 'Let's go outside. The sunset really is very beautiful.' She gestured for them to stand. 'It would be a shame to miss it. Then, perhaps, you can tell us what we need to know.'

Irina retrieved the couple's walking boots, which were drying out on a sheet of newspaper by the front door. She stood over them while they attempted to lace them up with shaking, clumsy fingers. 'That will do,' she said after a few moments. 'We are not going far.'

She opened the door and led them outside. The sun was setting fast now, racing towards a group of low islands: a deep purple swelling on the horizon.

'It is a good view. Those islands are the Hebrides?' Irina said, keeping her tone conversational as she led them across the springy grass, right up to the edge of the cliff.

Fiona Hicks wiped the tears away from her eyes. 'I don't know what this is about but please just leave us alone. We won't say anything.'

Irina patted Fiona on the back as if trying to reassure her. Then she grabbed a handful of the woman's fleece and pushed her a step closer to the sheer drop. Her feet scrabbled for purchase sending a shower of pebbles over the edge. Hicks moved towards her but Marshall grabbed his arm and bent it back up behind him until he yelped in pain. Oily black waves broke on the granite boulders that littered the beach twenty metres below. A lone gull cried out as if in warning.

'Fiona, please ask your husband to tell me where I can find his lover.'

'For Christ's sake,' shouted Hicks. 'I don't know where she is.'

'Steven,' said Fiona, her breathing ragged through the sobs. 'Please just tell her.'

'I don't know, Fiona. You have to believe me.'

Irina looked into his eyes. Whether or not Fiona believed him, she did. He knew nothing. Which was a shame as she'd been tasked to bring both Hicks and Sawyer.

'Please let her go,' said Hicks.

Irina smiled. 'Of course.' She let go of Fiona's fleece then shoved her in the small of the back, sending her over the edge. The piercing scream lasted barely two seconds before it was cut short. Marshall silenced Hicks's own screams with a savage crack over the back of the head with his gun. He laid the unconscious man on the grass as Irina leant out over the cliff until she could see Fiona Hicks's lifeless body rolling in the surf.

'Good,' she said. 'I'll go and pack his things while you put him in his car.'

CHAPTER 1

Three years inside is a long time for anyone. For an ex-policeman it's a lifetime.

Matt Curzon lay on his bunk looking up at the ceiling of his cell and listened to a fly as it bumped and buzzed against the glass of the tiny window, frantically seeking a way out, too stupid to find one. In his previous life on the outside, the fly would have been an irritant. And it would be dead by now. Here, on the inside, it was almost company.

He had spent all of the past thirty-six months two weeks and five days in the VP, or vulnerable prisoners' wing of the Segregation Unit. The wing was jokingly referred to by the prison community as 'Savile Row' because this was also where they housed the sex offenders. Sex offenders were right at the bottom of any prison's hierarchy. Unless, of course, there was an ex-cop in residence.

Curzon had had no choice but to accept his classification as a vulnerable prisoner and it meant almost complete isolation. Which was fine by him. He didn't want to talk to the other prisoners on the wing and they didn't want to talk to an ex-cop.

The monotony had not been broken by many visits either. His wife, Rachel, had come a few times in the first six months but on her last visit she had told him of her plans to move out, to start again. She would keep in touch for their son's sake but she didn't want an argument. He agreed. What was the point of more arguments? This had been coming for a long time and the prison sentence had just tipped the balance. His ex-colleagues had stayed away too. Not that he blamed them. They had their own careers to worry about and they wouldn't want to be seen fraternising with a criminal.

Curzon rolled off his bunk the moment he heard the door being unlocked and was already standing holding the black bin liner that held his few personal possessions by the time it swung open. The warder stood on the threshold, experienced enough to know never to enter a cell without backup. The warder's name was Houseman and he was the most senior of the regular staff in the Segregation Unit. He was about fifty, short but powerfully built. His face had a permanent scowl and he treated all the prisoners with the same open contempt.

'You ready?' Houseman asked.

Curzon took a last glance around his cell as if to make sure he hadn't forgotten anything. But aside from an iPod, a few well-thumbed paperbacks, several items of clothing and his wash kit, there was nothing to forget. Except the last three years, two weeks and five days.

Then something occurred to him.

He placed the bin liner on the floor, ignoring the heavy sigh from Houseman. He crossed to the window and reached up through the slot in the wire mesh. He opened the window as wide as it would go and used his other hand to shepherd the fly out through the gap. The room fell silent. He picked up his stuff again and nodded at Houseman. 'Ready,' he said.

Houseman moved aside to let him through the cell door then gestured for him to walk ahead along the corridor. He fell into step behind, his heavy boots keeping perfect time with the squeak that Curzon's own cheap trainers made on the polished vinyl floor. The air was heavy with the smell of industrial-strength cleaners, which still caught at the back of

Curzon's throat even after all this time.

The animal noises started long before they reached the scuffed pale blue door at the end of the corridor. The first prisoner's grunts were quickly taken up by the others on the wing. Curzon stopped and he felt Houseman's breath close to his ear.

'Keep going.'

Curzon ignored the warder. He turned to the nearest door and saw half a face pressed up against the wire-reinforced glass of the cell door, yellow teeth, thin lips and ruddy pock-marked skin.

'Pig,' the prisoner shouted between grunts, his rasping voice only slightly deadened by the heavy door.

Curzon smiled and shook his head, 'Not any more.'

'Move.'

Curzon felt Houseman putting a guiding hand on the small of his back. He was clearly anxious to get on. Curzon began walking again, the squeals and grunts echoing down the corridor like a busy morning at an abattoir.

Once the heavy steel door had slammed shut behind them, he was led away from the cell blocks to the lower security section of the prison. The corridors were the same white-painted brick but the doors lining them were wood instead of metal. He heard a sudden burst of laughter. It was probably a couple of off-duty warders sharing a joke, but the sound sent a shiver across his shoulders. He couldn't remember the last time he had laughed at anything.

After going through another security door, which Houseman unlocked by entering a code on a keypad, they emerged into a large, square, high-ceilinged room. There was a stainless steel counter on the left-hand side with an open door behind it and a door marked *Toilet* next to that. But it was the door opposite from where he now stood that had Curzon's full attention. It was on the back wall and had a small window set into it through which he could see sunlight. He turned as another warder appeared through the door behind the counter.

He was older than Houseman and his round face was red with the effort of carrying a large, white plastic box, which he dumped on the counter. He placed a padded envelope on its lid and slid the box towards Curzon.

'Check it's all there and sign here,' he said, taking a clipboard and pen from a hook on the back wall. He put it on the counter next to the box.

Curzon leant forward and signed without bothering to look in the box. 'I'm sure it's fine,' he said. 'Nothing worth stealing anyway.' Puzzled, he picked up the padded envelope and upended it. A set of house keys fell into his palm.

'From your wife's solicitor,' said the warder. 'Arrived last week.'

Curzon nodded, removed the lid of the box and reached inside. Lying on top was a folded black suit. It was the suit he had been wearing to court. And the suit he had worn to his wedding three years before that. It wasn't the only suit he owned but it was the only one he had that had been made-to-measure.

'You can change in there,' said Houseman, gesturing towards the toilet door.

Curzon left the two guards chatting about the hot weather and took his box inside the toilet. Beneath the suit he found the black leather holdall, which held the rest of his things. He unzipped it and pulled out a white shirt – it was a little wrinkled, and there was a ring of dirt inside the collar, but it would be fine under the suit jacket.

He stripped off his old faded jeans and blue T-shirt and got dressed. The suit still fitted well, although the shoulders felt a little tight. He had never had any problem with his weight and the bland prison food hadn't been much of a temptation. But with nothing else to do, he had spent as much time as he was allowed exercising in the gym.

After lacing up his black shoes, he retrieved his wallet from the bottom of the holdall along with his mobile phone. There was no point turning it on. The battery would be flat and the contract would have lapsed long ago. Besides, it wasn't as if anyone was going to call him.

He stuffed his books and wash things into the holdall along with the rest of his clothes then tossed the jeans, T-shirt and old trainers into the empty plastic box before returning to the main room.

Houseman and the other warder stopped talking as soon as they saw him. Houseman looked over, opened his mouth as if he was going to say something and then changed his mind.

'What?' asked Curzon. The other warder tried to hide a smile.

Houseman hesitated a moment longer, then seemed to come to a decision. 'You think you had it tough in here? What do you think will happen when Scoville finds out you're free?'

Curzon ignored the question but it was one he'd been asking himself over and over the last few weeks. He shrugged. 'If that's everything,' he said, 'I'd like to go now.'

The older warder handed him an envelope. 'Your paperwork.'

Curzon took the envelope and tucked it into his jacket pocket then followed Houseman across to the final door, the one with the window. He watched as he entered the code. There was a buzz as the electronic bolt disengaged and Houseman opened the door. Curzon stepped past him and out into the early morning sun.

'Watch your back, Curzon.'

Curzon paused at the top of the steps as the heavy wooden door slammed shut behind him, cutting off the laughter from the two men inside. He took a deep breath, filling his lungs with fresh air. Air that smelled of newly cut grass.

CHAPTER 2

Curzon walked up the road, checking the numbers of the doors as he went. It was an unremarkable London street lined with well-kept Victorian houses. These had mostly been turned into flats with the occasional 1950s purpose-built block, which had presumably sprung up from the rubble of wartime bombsites.

He paused outside number 48 and approached the two, black-painted doors marked A and B. His was the one on the left, 48 A. He dug around in his pocket for the keys, which the warder had handed to him that morning. As he slotted the key into the lock, he heard a car slow down. He glanced over his shoulder and saw it was a dark grey BMW. He watched as it slowly drove past, remembering Houseman's warning. The car didn't stop and, as it disappeared from view, he decided it was nothing to worry about. It was probably just a shopper looking for a parking space or one of his new neighbours showing an interest.

Curzon had never seen his flat before. He knew it only from the estate agent's blurb, which Rachel had read out to him on one of her early visits.

'This delightful two bedroom maisonette flat is on the ground floor of this newly refurbished Victorian house. Boasting a large open-plan reception room with high ceilings, period details, stylish integrated kitchen, contemporary bathroom and sole use of the pretty south-facing garden.'

After the trial Rachel had been too frightened to return to their old house in Ealing for fear that there might be reprisals from Scoville. He had, of course, agreed to put the small house, which his mother had left him, on the market and to use the money to buy this flat near Hammersmith.

Rachel had told him it was in the catchment area of a good primary school, which would be perfect for Sam when the time came. But the time never came. Once the estate agents and solicitors had done whatever estate agents and solicitors do to earn their percentage, when the house was sold and the contracts exchanged, Rachel had no need of it. She and Sam had already moved in with John Fielding.

Curzon pushed the door open against a drift of unopened mail and stepped inside. It was dusty and airless and the summer heat had turned it into an oven. He stepped over the mail and walked along the short, windowless corridor. The first door on his left revealed a small bathroom with a tiny window. At the end of the corridor were two more doors. The first led to a double bedroom with a window and a closed roller blind. He dropped his holdall onto the empty floor and went to explore the rest of the flat.

The sitting room led off the final door of the corridor and was large – as promised by the estate agent. Even so, most of the floor space was taken up with cardboard packing boxes. They had been dumped by the removal men in a haphazard fashion, stacked one on top of another. Some had sprung open but most remained sealed with brown sticky tape.

Like the bedroom, the blinds in this room were closed. He crossed to the closest window and released the roller. It clattered up and a shaft of sunlight shone across the polished wood floor, illuminating the dust in the air, which his presence had disturbed. A large tree stood in the far corner of the tiny rear garden and its leaves cast green dappled shadows into the flat.

Several dead flies lay on the sill, legs upwards. He unlocked the window, lifted the sash and brushed the dried husks outside. As he did so, he became aware of the white noise of children shouting and laughing somewhere in the distance. It took him a few moments to realise that the sound must be coming from the playground of the nearby primary school; the primary school Sam would be attending.

He returned to the bedroom and unzipped his holdall. He retrieved one of the paperbacks, his dog-eared French/English dictionary, and took it back to the main room, flicking through the pages. Midway in, he found the photograph he had tucked in there for safekeeping. He carefully peeled back the Blu Tack that held it in place and looked at it. The face of a happy, five-year-old boy smiled back at him.

He stepped around the worktop and into the kitchen area with its brand new built-in appliances. He stuck the photograph on the door of the fridge next to the instruction manual that was still taped there. He ripped off the manual then searched around for the plug and switched the fridge on. While it hummed into life, he noticed another door leading from the sitting room and opened it. It was a small box room. This, he realised with a sudden feeling of emptiness, would have been Sam's room.

He crossed to the window and released the blind. As he did so, he glanced out of the window. A dark grey BMW was parked outside. It looked like the same dark grey BMW as before and he could see two men sitting inside. The passenger was staring directly at him and for a brief moment, their eyes met.

Curzon ran out of the room and back along the corridor. He lost his footing slightly on the heap of mail and slammed into the door. Recovering, he wrenched it open and ran out to the pavement. The BMW pulled out with a short squeal and drove away.

'Wait,' shouted Curzon and started running down the centre of the street after it. The car began to pick up speed, lengthening the gap between them. There was a brief flare of brake lights as it reached the end of the road and then it was gone.

JENNIFER STONE

Jennifer Stone was born in Romford. In her writing, she is keen to celebrate her Essex heritage and traditions of her youth such as drinking alcopops and extreme eyebrow grooming. These days, she lives in Suffolk where she teaches English and acquires a tan naturally.

jstone53@msn.com

Cherry PI

18th August 2015

We'd spent the day slumped on the settee in front of the TV, only leaving it to go and get top-ups of Diet Coke and Doritos. I had Twitter running on my phone, Facebook on the iPad. The hot topic of conversation was who was going to be voted off that night and whether Jodrell Banks would manage to claw back her glamorous modelling career in light of having lost three stone with *Big Blubber*'s help.

'Her boobs'll be all saggy – just sayin',' said Kelsey who was doing a design on her toenails that involved four different bottles of polish balanced on the edge of my coffee table. 'She'll have to get implants and her whole thing is, that she's natural, innit?'

'Maybe she'll get a presenting job or something that doesn't require her to get them out,' I replied as I scanned Twitter for celebrity reactions to the fact that Fat Barry Island, the football commentator, lost five pounds overnight and was therefore that day's *Big Blubber* winner. This meant that he didn't have to do any exercise and could have a steak for his lunch. The others carped and whined that Fat Barry has somehow cheated the system. *#fatbarrysdiet* was trending and a few diet experts were commenting that it wasn't possible to lose that much weight in one day.

We were only involved in this marathon *Big Blubber* binge because our friend from school, Kenny Thorpe, was on the show. He had enjoyed brief success with his indie band before piling on eight stone, so he qualified to appear as a contestant. Miraculously, despite being the most miserable celebrity on it, he'd survived the public vote to get down to the final five.

We watched him arguing with two of the other contestants: Dion and Drew. They were trying to persuade him to come to lunch as the rules of the show didn't permit skipping meals. He lay on his bed and refused to move, saying, 'Fuck off, you fat fuckers.' Unfortunately, these were the last words he said.

'Would you ever go on a show like that? I couldn't bear all them cameras on me all the time. I don't know why Kenny went on there,' said Kelsey, frowning as she concentrated on her phone and her little toenail at the same time.

'No me neither, he probably needs the money,' I offered. 'Even if I was desperate for cash, I'd rather poke my own eyes out than do that. People are so judgy.' I stuffed another handful of Doritos in my mouth, glad that there was no one apart from Kelsey to see me. 'I can't believe I used to go out with Kenny, he's so blatantly gay. Have you seen the way he's been flirting with X?'

Kelsey snorted and started snapping photos of her toes for Instagram. 'Fat lot a good that'll do 'im. Hasn't that X got no genitals or something?'

'No Kels, they're not a hermaphrodite, they're non-binary.'

'Right. And that means…?'

'Er, that they don't, like, feel that they're man or lady?'

'Right. Like one a them Thai ladyboys they had on at The Brentwood Centre?'

My attention was suddenly dragged back to the screen as I saw some vigorous movement; X was leaning over Kenny's bed and was shaking Kenny, their hands covered in what looked like red paint. They began screaming and banging on the two-way mirrors, spreading the red stuff around. The camera jerked wildly around, focusing on the floor but the sound hadn't caught up and X's screaming was still audible for a couple of seconds after the screen went black and the Channel 6 logo appeared. I turned, stunned, to Kelsey.

'Did you see that? What the fuck just happened?'

'Was that blood?'

'I dunno, I was talking to you and then like, X is shaking Kenny and saying he's dead.'

'They wasn't saying he was dead, they was giving it "help me, help me"!'

'Quick, rewind it. Where's the remote?'

Kelsey jumped up, knocked over all of the nail polish and smudged her entire left foot. She found the remote down the side of the TV. 'I swear, they was like literally sayin', "help me"!'

'They so wasn't. They was shouting, "he's dead!"'

I jabbed at the remote but for some reason, it wouldn't go back. Our phones leapt alive in a chorus of beeps and pings but I was too shocked and shaky to pick mine up. I was trying to convince myself that it was some sort of trick or stunt and that we hadn't been watching properly.

However, as the rest of the evening on Channel 6 and every other media outlet unfolded, it became clear; whatever the differences were between what we thought we'd seen, one thing was certain: Kenny Thorpe was dead.

CHAPTER ONE

20th July 2017

Caravan Has Lost Its Way – *by Julia Andrews*
It seems that Channel 6 has hit an all-time low with its latest 'celebrity' show, The Caravan of Love. *Who would have thought that packing 10 Z-list celebs off to a caravan park in Rhyl would be entertainment for anyone daft enough to tune in? The producers of this lame reality show, that's who. This pathetic excuse of a programme makes Channel 6's previously dire primetime offering* Obese, Poor and Stripping for Cash *seem like a masterclass in cutting-edge documentary making.*

COL *attempts to match stars with 'commoners' by forcing them to shack up in caravans together. It seemed for a while that likeable investigative reporter for* Look East *and* The Essex Chronicle, *Cherry Hinton, who, up until now was best known for her work on the Troy Hatton case, had found love in the arms of chirpy city boy Patrick Boughton. However, it appears that the double-crossing, double D 'journalist' had other ideas and was on the show to play an entirely different game.*

Channel 6 has a history of making shocking reality shows and, after the horror of 2015's Big Blubber, *they will have been keen to avoid the kind of controversy that Hinton's antics courted. One can only wonder at what she was thinking.*

—

'All right that's enough thanks! I thought you said you'd found a review to cheer me up! How is that supposed to make me feel better? And what's she doing writing about it *now* – I got kicked off about four months ago? I never liked her; she well thought she was all that cos she worked for *The Sun*!'

'Well at least she said you was likeable. *The Mirror* said you was a scheming cow who deserved nothing more than a lifetime of obscurity.'

Kelsey folded the paper in half and placed it back on the counter. I sighed and picked at the skin around my nails; I *wanted* a lifetime of obscurity.

'And don't do that neither, you'll make it look all skanky and then no one'll wanna buy your cakes *or* see you on the telly.'

She glanced down at her own perfect nails which, in honour of it being summer, were decorated with jaunty beach hut style stripes. Kelsey was a true nail artist and I suddenly felt awkward with my amateurish cakes sitting next to her. I could feel tears welling up again and fought to swallow them down. She noticed and glared at me.

'Now's not the time for self-pity Cherry, look when Joe dumped me, I felt really crap but I didn't stay in and let my eyes get all puffy, did I? No. I said to myself, now is the time to take *Nails by Kelsey* to the high street. This shop you've got Cherry, it's an opportunity!'

I looked around at my tiny cupcake shop, nestled between *New Look* and some shop that was forever closing down. I'd done my best; the window was rammed full of my speciality cupcakes and the glass shelves were polished to perfection or were, until Kelsey had found her way in and smeared her perfectly tipped fingers all over my counter. I absent-mindedly added a Vajazzled Muffin to the stand on the counter which I had labelled the Essex Collection and turned it round so the sequins caught the light.

'I love your new sign, babe, it looks well classy with them light bulbs,' said Kelsey, still trying to cheer me up. 'What you need though, is some of them two dots.'

I sighed. We'd been over this about twenty times. Even my dad, the shop's 'real' owner, had tried to convince me. Personally, I think this was to assuage his hurt feelings after I insisted we ditch *Len and Maureen's cakes, bread and pastry products* for something a bit more catchy – *Cherry's Cupcakes*.

'It's a colon and it's pointless. You don't need a colon in the middle of your shop name.'

'But Hair by Jo:anne's got one. It looks *well* more classy.'

It looked as though I would have to resign myself to being less classy than the rest of Brentwood High Street.

I could live with that.

'Look, Kels, I know what you're saying but I can't have a sign that's not orthographically accurate.'

'Oh, right,' said Kelsey, losing interest since I wasn't to be swayed on the matter. She inspected the tray of cakes I was in the process of decorating. 'Are them ones for the police party you was talking about? Here, that Jacob Stow might come in to collect them, eh?' She winked and attempted to elbow me in the ribs across the counter. Failing, she caught her sleeve in a Raspberry Writtle Flapjack balanced on my Essex Collection stand and ended up with a smear of jammy icing halfway up her Moschino-clad arm. My stomach clenched when she mentioned Jacob. He'd barely spoken to me since the show.

'He's not even been in the shop to say hello, I don't think he'll be coming in to collect cakes off me.'

'Yeah... well you say that, but... he might've split up with that skinny model. And now you're a big star and all it could be, like, he's interested in you again.'

'I *told* you, I really genuinely liked Patrick and I don't think being kicked off a telly programme and losing your job in the process makes you irresistible.' Especially to successful, good-looking (and very vain) men like Jacob. Kelsey looked at me pityingly; she'd known me since we were in Sixth Form College and therefore knew all about my history with Jacob Stow.

Jacob Stow was the so-called 'hunky star' of Channel 6's 'reality' crime show, You're Nicked, and was also Brentwood Police force's local spokesman for all things reality related. His arrest two years ago of 'Fat' Barry Island, following the murder of Kenny Thorpe, had made him almost a national celebrity. Indeed, my Stow-away Secret Filling Cupcakes had been flying off the shelves as quickly as I could make them. But, that didn't necessarily mean that I wanted him to come in and see a cupcake with his face on it for sale. He had plenty of reasons to dislike me already and I didn't want to add to them.

Unfortunately, despite his having a range of qualities that would repulse any woman in her right mind, I also harboured a massive, unrequited crush on Jacob that I had been carrying round with me pointlessly, like a barren womb, since I was sixteen. Ten long years, the crush had festered and rotted until I was left in a perpetual state of both hating and loving him.

'Now,' she continued, 'my next lady is in at 11.30 but I'll see you later.'

I loved the way she said this as though she hadn't rocked up with a mug and a torn-out article from The Sun an hour ago and demanded a coffee from my tiny kitchen out the back and one of my Cheese and Basildon Scones to go with it. But I suppose friends are there to forget your failings.

I stood behind the counter suddenly feeling terribly alone. The shop was as good as I could make it in the few weeks I had to prepare between taking out the loan and reopening as the all-new *Cherry's Cupcakes*. The bank had given us only one month to get up and running before we had to start paying them back. I insisted on the revamp. If we were going to be successful, we couldn't keep on doing the same old thing and losing business to places like *Greggs* and our arch rivals, *The Quid Bakery*.

I'd changed everything about the grimy little shop that carried with it the air of a seventies vegan retreat and tried to make it feel both glamorous and welcoming with lots of lights, painted tongue and groove panelling and a diner style floor. The shelves gleamed with Essex-themed cakes and business had been fairly brisk in my first few weeks of opening.

I wasn't naïve though; I knew some people were coming in to catch a glance of the 'Cherry Hinton' who'd fallen so spectacularly from grace just months before. But I was doing my best to get up again.

CHAPTER TWO

The door swung open. She didn't look like she came from Brentwood; her skin was pale and you could see pores and flaws clearly. She had eyebrows that were constructed of only hair. She approached the counter with an almost furtive look. 'Serial Dieter' was my first instinct. Probably on the wagon at the moment but my chocolate Vajazzled Muffin in the window had sent her over the edge.

I smiled my special customer service smile and said, 'Y'aright babes, what can I get you?'

She glanced about her, as if she were checking that no one was going to suddenly spring from the kitchen. She leant in so close that I could see she wasn't wearing any foundation and she started tugging the sleeves of her jumper down over her hands in a nervous gesture. She looked both strange and familiar at the same time.

She said, in a voice made croaky by anxiety and overuse, 'Are you Cherry Hinton?'

I laughed but it was just a laughing sound.

'You must be one of the only people in Brentwood who *needs* to ask that question.'

'Well, I wasn't sure, you've changed a lot.'

Confused, I replied, 'What since February?'

Confusion crossed her face now, 'What do you mean? I saw you on *Look East* last year but the last time I *saw you* saw you was about 10 years ago. You look loads better now though.'

'Umm thanks,' I replied, not really sure where this conversation was going but glad that there was no reference to *The Caravan of Love*. Yet.

'Look, I've heard that you, like, find things out for people. Y'know things that the police won't help you with. I saw you on that programme, *Troy Hatton Literally Exposed.* How on earth did you manage to get him to take all his clothes off on camera?'

I felt my face grow hot. Oh good, I was blushing at the memory of asking a crazed criminal to show me his 'sexy tattoos' in the name of investigative journalism. Coughing, I answered my visitor with a vague, 'Er... must be my charm or something. Anyways, I don't mean to be rude but I feel like I ought to know you...'

'Oh, yeah, sorry. I thought you might've recognised me. I'm Brooke Thorpe.'

Brooke Thorpe. The name sounded vaguely familiar but I couldn't place it. I was going to have to style it out and pretend I knew her. Then I remembered. She was Kenny Thorpe's sister.

No one really prepares you for a social situation in which you face the relatives of people murdered on live television. It was one of those things where anything I said would sound crass and wrong but not saying anything would be equally awkward. I kept it standard.

'Brooke, I'm so sorry to hear what happened to Kenny.'

She shrugged my pity off casually with the air of one who is tired of it.

'Yeah... well... happens, dunnit?'

It appeared that she had moved to the 'acceptance' part of the grieving process.

'What can I do for you?' I ventured.

At this, her face crumpled and she dug in her bag for a tissue. She shook her head, trying to speak and not cry at the same time. She managed neither and stood swaying, with big tears splashing on to my freshly mopped floor. I dragged Kelsey's stool round from my side of the counter and guided Brooke gently to it. Then, I reached into my under counter fridge and pulled out two bottles of Blue WKD. Popping the tops off,

I dropped a straw in each and slid one across the counter to Brooke who was dabbing in her eyes and scrubbing at her nose with the tissue.

I quickly drew the bolt across the front door and turned the sign around to 'closed'. I gave her my best warm and empathetic smile, 'Why don't you tell me what it is, babes?'

She took a long hard gulp of Blue WKD and replied in a way that made me think it was rehearsed, 'So, everyone knows it was Fat Barry, don't they? I mean everyone sees him lean over Kenny and he's still alive wiv his legs moving and that. Then he's dead. Right?'

The tone of this final question dared me to disagree with her. I nodded to appear wise.

'Poor Kenny. But I don't see how...'

She interrupted me with a lot more force than was suggested by her swaying sniffing form.

'Look you found out what Troy Hatton was up to – didn't you? I saw you on *Look East* and everything. And what about all them stories in the *Chronicle*? "Our top reporter, Cherry Hinton, gets to the heart of the crime." That was you, wasn't it? Getting to the heart of the crime! The police, they're well pleased, all the glory for collaring Barry. But here's the thing, right, what if it weren't *Barry*?'

This all came out in a garbled rush but the poor woman didn't realise that I wasn't the same person she'd seen on *Look East* and that the *Chronicle* were denying that I'd ever worked for them.

Clearly, she'd not been watching *The Caravan of Love* or there'd be no way she'd want the help of, as the *Daily Star* had so pleasantly put it, 'Cheating slut-rat Cherry Hinton'. I opened my mouth to reply but as I did, we were both shocked by a frantic banging on the shop window. I turned to see a gang of Lycra-clad girls peering through the window. Once they'd clocked that it was indeed me, they screamed in unison, in what was supposed to be an impersonation of my voice saying what was apparently my catchphrase, 'What do you think you're playing at?' and ran giddily screeching down the road as fast as, I assumed, their cheap imitation Ugg boots would allow them. I moved back, ready to continue my conversation.

Brooke smiled sympathetically at me, 'Does that happen a lot?'

I shrugged again; it was tailing off. Straight after I'd been kicked out, it had been every hour or so. People had been banging on Mum and Dad's front door and throwing stuff. Some freaks even tried proposing and shoving bunches of flowers from the Esso garage through the letter box. On occasion even my friends did it. Now, a couple of days could go by without anyone mentioning it. In some ways, being shouted at in the shop was better than people coming to the house.

'What do you mean – what if it wasn't Barry? Everyone could see it was him.'

She side-eyed me and let out a sigh. She picked up her bag and started pushing the stool back, her mouth was pursed. She shook her head theatrically.

'I really thought you'd be different. I thought after all that shit with the shit-hole of love or whatever it's called, *you'd* at least understand that not everything you see is necessarily what's going on, but you're just the same as everyone else; like that guy on *Catchphrase*, "just say what you fucking see" – you're like a sheep.'

I felt my hackles rise and I stood up.

'Hang on a minute, before you start accusing me of being Roy Walker. An arrest was made; the evidence was there; Fat Barry didn't put up any kind of defence. It's hardly bloody obvious that there was a miscarriage of justice.' She scowled at me and I continued. Calmer this time. 'All right, I'm listening. What makes you think it's not him?'

She put her bag down on the counter and rummaged through it, pulling out a letter that was greasy and crumpled with being re-read. She thrust it at me.

'Here, read that and tell me what you reckon.'

So I did.

—

Dear Brooke,

Firstly, I imagine that this comes as somewhat of a shock but I urge you to continue reading prior to discarding this missive.

I have been handed a death sentence; not by Judge Marshall but by my doctor. It seems that I have only a few months left before I succumb to that most modern of plagues – cancer. The irony being, that had I not gone into The Big Blubber House and lost 8 stone, the tumour would have lain undetected and my death would have been a surprise to all, including me. I am thankful then, for the time left to me to make good my departure.

I would like you to know that I am an innocent man. I did not murder

your brother despite all appearances to the contrary. I can offer no further
explanation besides the fact I am content with the choices I have made and the
hand of fate that has delivered me to this place.

    Kindest regards,

    Barry Island

—

Well.

    Shit.

    'Brooke, when did you receive this?'

    'He's dead if that's what you're asking. He died last week in hospital. That's why I've come. I know he's dead but what if some fat bastard is walking around thinking they've got away with it? I need to know.'

    I could see what she was saying; the whole tone of the letter raised questions. It felt calm, and maybe I was romanticising deathbed epistles, but who would bother with something like that when they knew they were on their way out, unless it were true?

    'I totally hear you Brooke, I really do, but what do you want *me* to do about it?'

    All of my brain was telling me to give her a gift box of cupcakes and wish her luck. There was nothing that I could do. But my heart was pounding with excitement in a way that I hadn't felt for ages. Certainly, a long time before I was walked out of Enfys Holiday Park into a barrage of cameras and boos from Welsh and Liverpudlian scallies behind barriers. Where I was told by the shouty presenter, 'Bubbly' Bonny Rigg, that I was a liar and a cheat who ought to be ashamed of herself whilst the images from said 'interview' were being beamed live into homes around the UK including those of my friends and family. My silence and bowed head were interpreted by all the papers the following morning as 'chilling' and 'psychopathic'.

    It was as though Brooke sensed that I was hovering between saying yes and sending her on her way. She pressed me, 'Look, you're an investigator. I know it's all gone to shit after that programme you was on but you could help me. The police couldn't care less – it was their big conviction; they're not going to start poking around. Everyone's gunna think I'm the hysterical sister who can't face the fact that Barry's only served a year of his sentence. But you – you're cool and rational, just a journalist who's reviewing the case. Look, Cherry, I just want to *know.*'

The 'cool and rational' part of me kicked in at this point. 'Brooke, what if it *was* Barry? I don't want you to...'

She cut in, clearly having been prepared for my misgivings, 'Look, if it *was* Barry, there's no harm done is there?'

I didn't agree but I nodded anyway. I had more issues with this task. 'Brooke, won't this just rake...'

She read me again.

'Yes, it will rake it all up but I can take it. It can't hurt any worse the second time. Surely?'

I sighed. I really wanted to forget that I'd ever had any hopes and dreams beyond a shop rammed with Essex-based cakes and an occasional angry glare from Jacob through the window. I'd promised my mum and dad that I would focus on this and keep my head down for a while. But Brooke had definitely prepared for this conversation. Her whole manner had changed over the course of our conversation, from shaky sleeve puller to confident; cocky almost. It was this cocky, sly look that moved around the shop taking everything in. She looked at me straight.

'I got an enormous pay-out from Channel 6. Like, obscene amounts of cash to basically pipe down and not go blarting about it on *Mouthy and Menopausal*. I can pay you for your time.'

'Brooke, please, I don't want your money.'

'Mate, it's Channel 6's blood money. Call it an investment in the business or whatever. Don't be proud. It's not worth it.'

I hated talking about money; it made me squirm to be trying to thrash out a deal.

'OK, well let me start to look into things and we can discuss it when I actually start getting somewhere.'

She smiled and shrugged with raised eyebrows. I sensed that she understood but didn't agree.

'Cool. I've got a list here of the other four contestants; the two cameramen and the woman who was on *Big Blubber*'s voice duty. Oh, and the director of the show. I thought that'd be enough to be getting on with.'

She handed me the neatly handwritten piece of paper and her contact details. Before I had time to reflect on how confident she'd been that I would agree, she was gone.

I was still ruminating on who to interview first the following morning, as I balanced a large Tupperware on my hip with one hand and attempted to open the numerous locks on the front door with the other. A leaflet with *The Pie Shop* and *K9 Fashions* on the front caught my eye. A thick red line was drawn through the photos and beneath them read the caption, *Keep Brentwood For Real People*. It appeared that Councillor Boris O'Kane was escalating his campaign to get rid of reality stars' shops from the high street. Thankfully, I'd escaped his notice so far – probably because *Len and Maureen's Cakes* had been the least glamorous and superficial shopfront in Brentwood.

The only letters I got nowadays were from the bank, reminding me how much the business owed them, and of the stringent terms of the loan we took out to attempt to do up the tired pine kitchen look that my parents had favoured until a month ago. That's why the leaflet caught my eye so quickly.

I put down the cakes that I was trying to keep level – they'd taken me and mum until eleven to get just right – and opened up my laptop. When they weren't too busy trying to troll me on Twitter or Facebook, there were the occasional cards from psychos telling me how much they liked my breasts and what they would like to do to me if, for some reason, I lost my mind and met with them for the night of passion they were suggesting. However, these had tailed off in the last month or so.

An email with the title, *Kenny Thorpe*, caught my eye.

Cherry Hinton, stay out of business that doesn't concern you. Let fat blokes lie and get on with baking. Don't say you weren't warned. You're better off not getting involved.

A lump rose in my throat – I thought that I was getting better at dealing with stuff like this; like I said to Brooke, I'd had a lot worse in the first few weeks. But this was different. It felt really precise and careful; not the rantings of a nutter. More to the point, how did they even know about the conversation I'd had with Brooke the day before?

I tried not to think about it. After all, I had a hundred Glam Gypsy Wedding Cupcakes to ice before lunchtime.

But the email was still preying on my mind as I mixed my silver buttercream and ferreted in the storage area for the edible sequins I'd ordered specially for this project. Traveller community chic was all the rage for this year (so I kept telling my new clients) and I was hoping that if this one went well, I'd get some more orders.

After I had turned the *open* sign on the shop door, and arranged my Hornchurches of Plenty in the window, my thoughts turned back to Kenny Thorpe. I set about scrolling through my contacts on my phone, racking my brain to think who might a) know something, b) not hate me enough to share what they knew. The list was very short.

What I really wanted to know and, before the whole *Caravan* fiasco, could easily have found out, was what the police knew and what they had done about it. Unfortunately, my friendly contact in the police, Jacob, was now one of my biggest detractors.

S.W. HUDSON

S.W. Hudson was a finance director before turning to writing. He has had a lifelong interest in crime fiction and has always wanted to write a crime novel. He first studied creative writing through the Open University, before enrolling on the MA Crime Fiction course at UEA.

shane.horsell@btinternet.com

The Daisy Chain

Thursday, September 28th, 2017

I sit on a bench beneath the long horizontal bough of an ancient cedar of Lebanon, staring across Bentham Lake, trying to enjoy the last rays of the setting sun. Normally I would feel the sun's warmth, but today I feel nothing.

Anyone observing me over the last forty years would have seen that each evening I complete the same walk around the lake. I sit on the same bench, I run my hand over the same inscription on the bench, and then I smile. But over the last two weeks the smile has been absent, replaced with a deeply worried frown. I put my head in my hands. Why now? Why after all this time?

For anyone else the lake is a picture of tranquillity. Its surface perfectly still, reflecting three cumulous clouds that remain in the rose-coloured glow of the evening sky. A time traveller, miraculously transported from the eighteenth century to the twenty-first, would not notice any difference in the landscape. Nothing here has been changed by Man during that time; a natural paradise has evolved. The trees have grown. Moorhens, herons and kingfishers have made the lake their home; barn owls, nightjars, woodpeckers and nightingales have moved into the surrounding woods. Insects buzz everywhere and wildflowers grow in great billowing drifts.

I would like the whole Bentham Estate to be remembered for what it is: one of the last remaining unspoilt landscapes in England. Capability Brown himself planned the planting of weeping willows, wellingtonia and cedars all along the banks. Then the Estate's owner left things alone. Mother Nature can do great things if left alone for just five years; given two hundred and fifty years, it can create paradise on Earth and for me this is paradise.

All over Britain sprawling towns have been built on green fields, endless streams of cars pollute the air, chemicals are sprayed on fields killing all the flowers and insects. Surely these are far greater crimes than the one single crime committed here?

Bentham Estate may be my paradise but it's also my prison. Knowing what I know, how can I leave? Someone had to make sure the lake's secret was never revealed, and up until now, I had succeeded. Tomorrow I fear this may all change. If the secret is discovered, pictures of the Estate will be all over the television and the newspapers – a place where long ago a hideous crime was once carried out.

It all started to unwind when the Estate's owner ordered the lake to be desilted. Two hundred and fifty years of silt carried in by the stream had reduced the depth of the lake, and last year's drought showed just how shallow the water was in places. It did look unsightly, though a few more years wouldn't have harmed anybody...

But no, the owner ordered in the contractors. Give him his due, he planned the whole project carefully, even paid for large aerated tanks to rescue the fish. The outflow dam has been cut as low as possible to enable almost all of the water to escape. This allows the very deepest water to be dredged of silt – even more bad news for me. Just what I didn't want.

The contractors came two weeks ago armed with JCB diggers and a fleet of dumper trucks to carry the rich silt away to the pastures. They started at the shallow end of the lake where the stream enters. My peaceful haven of water and wood, where the heady scents of water mint and wild garlic usually fill the air, turned quickly into a noisy, muddy, diesel-smelling work site. But that was the least of my worries.

Today the workers have reached the deepest area of the lake, opposite the boathouse, the area I know holds the secret. Tomorrow it may be discovered and my world will never be the same again.

I am so deep in my own thoughts that I haven't even noticed that the clear evening air has rapidly cooled. Spiralling columns of mist are rising from the lake's surface. All is quiet, as if ancient magic is at work and ghosts are rising from the lake. Finally I stir from my thoughts. I read the inscription on the bench for one last time:

In loving memory of a wonderful girl, Daisy Spence 1959–1976,
you will never ever be forgotten.

I walk away into the wood, head bowed.

Friday, September 29th, 2017

This morning I rise early to watch their operations closely; hidden in the woods, just a shadowy figure. Just in case I am seen, I have binoculars around my neck, and a rucksack on my back containing a bird field guide, flask of tea and sandwiches. If anyone does approach me, I can claim to be some mad keen ornithologist.

I know there is still a slim chance the lake's secret will remain undiscovered. Maybe it has sunk so deep in the silt that the JCB's jaws will miss it, or maybe the silt is so thick that no one will spot it when it does get lifted out, amongst all that mud. There is still a chance.

I'm on edge; in contrast I can see the job has long since become routine for the contractors. The dumper truck drivers line up behind the three JCBs ready to receive their next load of silt. I watch transfixed as one of the JCB drivers reaches the deepest part of the lake, in front of the boathouse. This is the area, the danger zone.

The JCB has to be careful in its manoeuvres, as just here, the original stream bed is a couple of feet deeper than anywhere else on the lake. I watch intently as its caterpillar belt is challenged by the layers of silt, as if the lake is fighting back, trying to hold onto its secret. After slipping and tottering precariously the JCB finally finds traction on the gravel beneath. Its driver reaches further and further away from the bank, the mouth of the JCB plunging into the water, looking like a long extinct, garish yellow dinosaur. The bucket tilts, picking up its muddy cargo and then the vast neck and head of the machine swivels, spewing its contents into the waiting dumper truck. Six times it does this before the truck is full. The truck reverses out and sloshes away, water escaping from its front as it bounces across the rutted field.

I watch for the next hour or so, as the giant machine continues removing more and more silt from the lake. The day has warmed up and I take off my jumper, placing it on the cracked woodland floor. Now more than ever I can't afford to take my eyes off the JCB. I unscrew my flask and sit back against a tree trunk, sipping my tea slowly. After half an hour I am down to the last dregs and I'm trying hard not to allow my hopes to rise. Maybe the JCB has missed it.

I look across as the JCB reaches further out, scooping deep into the sediment. As it swivels around, water and liquid mud fall, and there hanging, half in and half out of the bucket is something solid. Is it a rock or part of a tree stump long since submerged? Then I see what looks like a piece of rope hanging down. It must be the ex-army holdall. Has the driver spotted it? The JCB turns and tilts, the object falls into the waiting truck, and the JCB swivels away and starts reaching into the lake again. My luck is in; the JCB driver hasn't noticed it. I switch my attention to the dumper truck driver; he has his headphones on and looks in a world of his own. I haven't really planned this next move. I always thought if anything was found, it would be obvious to the workers – now I know there is a real chance. I can mentally note where the truck driver drops the load and then go back this evening to recover the holdall and hide it, until I can safely put it back into the lake.

I pick up my flask and make my way up the pasture. Behind me the truck accelerates up the incline, approaching the top of the field. It finds an area of clean grass and tilts up. The holdall hits the grass amongst all the thick black mud and water. The driver reverses back and then stops. He gets out of his cab. I can feel my heart almost pounding out of my chest. He must have spotted it. He takes two steps into the mud and heaves the sack out, before going to his cab and returning with a pair of shears. He cuts away at the rope which holds the neck of the holdall together. I find myself running towards the scene, still just inside the woods. I watch as the rope is cut. The driver turns the holdall upside down and empties its contents onto a patch of clean grass.

A house brick falls out, then another. Then a clatter of what looks like bones, human bones. The driver steps back and drops the sack. I hear him gasping for breath. He waves down one of the other dumper truck drivers who joins him staring at the bones. I am close enough to hear their conversation.

'Tell me.... Please tell me they're not human bones?'

'No, I don't think so, there's no human skull, probably just the farmer drowning a fox or something.'

Now a couple of the other dumper truck drivers notice the stoppage – they're always looking for any excuse to stop work. Soon, much to my annoyance, several of the team are clustered around the bones. I listen to the comments, not knowing what to do next. My brain has frozen. The lake's secret is there in front of them.

'That's human. Looks like a rib cage.'

'Perhaps the skull is in all that mud somewhere. Or maybe someone was beheaded.'

Now there are six of the team clustered around. I back away further behind a tree trunk.

'I wonder how long they've been in there?'

'Could've been centuries, lots of people chopping each other's heads off then.'

'Not with that string attached lad, that's synthetic. Maybe the old squire has knocked off one of the maids.'

'Not sure he could catch them.'

Someone laughs. I feel sick.

I notice the site manager has joined the group and I hear a phone call made to Cirencester police station, who are quickly on the scene, all flashing blue lights; as the police arrive I disappear into the shadows.

THE ENQUIRY

Friday, September 29th, 2017

My name is Chief Inspector Liz Glover. I was the first detective on the scene. I made sure I was the first detective on the scene – that was no lucky coincidence. As soon as I heard about the bones being found in Bentham Lake, I knew it must be her; poor Daisy Spence. Forty-one years after going missing, finally, we had found her.

My interest in this case runs deep. That is a serious understatement. It is in my blood. It has made me what I am today. Let me explain.

Daisy's disappearance was one of the few cases my father was unable to solve. A rare blot, on a near-perfect, forty-year career with the Gloucestershire Constabulary. The Daisy Spence case affected him, more than he would ever admit. It changed him almost beyond recognition, and it changed the way he was towards me.

In 1976 he was a Detective Inspector; happy with his lot, a fun-loving family man. Serious crimes didn't happen in this part of the world. He'd tell me that London bobbies transferring to Gloucestershire would laugh at the headlines from the local paper: *Cows on road cause traffic chaos* or *Swarming bees cause fête to be abandoned*.

Then Daisy disappeared.

At seventeen, she was two years older than me. A plain-looking girl, just like me, and Dad became convinced I would be next. Suddenly I had to be indoors by nine, never out alone and certainly not allowed to play in the fields. My idyllic world had become like Colditz, overnight. My dad was certain Jack the Ripper himself was stalking the honey-coloured villages and golden fields of the Cotswolds. Hiding behind every Jersey cow, fluffy sheep or stone wall was a crazed madman.

Saturday May 8th 1976 was the day our world changed. Maybe now it could change again, this time for the better. Maybe we have found her and all the questions can be answered. No longer will she be a missing person, someone who might have run off to London or gone abroad. No longer will she be a suspected suicide: someone who wasted all her potential; someone who, in a dark depression, took her own life. No. This much I already know: suicides don't chop their own heads off, climb into a sack with some bricks and throw themselves deep into a lake. She was murdered and now I am heading up a manhunt.

Instinctively I know this is my career-defining case. Nothing before or after will matter. This is my fate. The reason I was born. The reason I became a copper.

On finding the bones, the one person I had to tell first was Dad, hoping it might bring him peace of mind at last, and freedom. Freedom from his guilt at not finding Daisy nor whoever was responsible for her murder. Whilst some in the force were convinced she had run away, he was always convinced she had been murdered.

He still has connections in the force. If I wanted to be the one to tell him first, I needed to head up there straight away. As a bonus, it was Friday, which meant fish and chips, proper homemade chips, unless the menu had changed, but that hadn't happened in my lifetime.

Mum and Dad still live in the house that I grew up in. Tucked away on a lane, halfway to nowhere. It was built in the 1930s, now looking more rundown than I've noticed before, with a garden that tells of owners who know their plants, but now don't have the energy to keep them in check. It's a garden I played in as a child with my friends and a garden in which I know all the best hiding places. I know where the robin nests every spring, I know which windows let the draughts in. I know where to read in the evening and catch the last of the setting sun. I contemplated all this and more as I walked up to the front door, lost in a nostalgic haze. I let myself in and went into the lounge.

'Hello love,' Mum was knitting in her armchair. 'We're having dinner in a bit. Do you want me to put something on for you?'

'Do I ever say no?'

Mum went out into the kitchen. Dad had been reading a book but put it down. 'What brings you out here to see us? Not much happening on the serious crime front?'

'Funny you should say that.' I wanted to slow myself down. I wanted to string it out. Just like he would have done to me, but I failed.

'We've made a discovery up at Bentham.'

He normally has some comment to make but not this time.

'Don't get your hopes up, but when they were desilting the lake, they've found a holdall with bones inside.'

Dad stared into the three orange bars glowing on the electric fire.

'Daisy?' was all he said. All he needed to say.

'We don't know for sure yet. There's no skull, but they've been in the water for an awfully long time. The pathologist's report will hopefully be ready tomorrow.'

I saw his eyes; watery, full of emotion. I looked away. I wasn't sure I could watch my seventy-nine-year-old father cry, but when he spoke his voice was still strong and purposeful.

'It can only be her. Thank the Lord. I thought I'd go without knowing the answer.'

'Don't be stupid. You've got years left yet, and more to the point, I hope you've still got all your marbles. Because I'm going to need your help.'

'You don't need me, you've got younger and better brains than mine there now. Anyway all our old stuff is in the files.'

'Yes, but I'd rather have it all first hand. Tell me about it – what do you remember?'

Mum came back in with a mug of tea and some biscuits.

Dad got up and walked to the large lounge window and looked out. I dunked a malted milk biscuit and watched him. I know his habits almost as well as my own and I knew his reply when it came would be the full story, nothing missed.

'It's one of those days I'll never forget. You know like the day you were born or the day I married your mother. I've relived it often enough. Sometimes I've tried to forget it, but I know I'll never be able to.

'It was warm, really warm for May. I can remember it was the anniversary of VE day. We should have been out celebrating, instead we were looking for a missing girl. She had missed all her lessons on the Friday, no one had seen her since the Thursday evening and she hadn't told anyone or left any note to say she was going away. We had thirty bobbies out looking for her.

You know what it's like; the first twenty-four hours are the critical ones. We searched Bentham Woods, Monkswood's grounds and the surrounding fields. It was so hot we were all in shirtsleeves. The may blossom had just come fully out and it filled the air with this sweet aroma. Before that day I'd always loved that smell, but since, it's always reminded me of Daisy.

'We interviewed so many people: pupils of Monkswood, teachers, everyone up at Bentham, even some gypsies that had camped on the roadside. I still remember clearly what an old gypsy woman said, "What do you expect, the may blossom is out." Apparently in the old days, during the May Day celebrations, a May Queen was crowned with may blossom, before being ritually slaughtered.

'We did everything we possibly could. We looked everywhere and asked all her friends but no one knew where she was. The following day the divers went into the lake and found nothing. Bad job they must have done.'

'What was Daisy like?'

'According to the head, she was a clever girl, best in the year in most of her subjects. She may have had the cards stacked against her from an early age; you remember she was an orphan?'

I nodded.

'But she applied herself in whatever she did. A really good tennis player, very good at netball and lacrosse too. Apparently she got on well with all of the teachers, which is what you'd expect with her attitude. They said she loved her schoolwork, so much so, she would see some of the teachers outside of her normal classes. Any of them could have had designs on her or even been having an affair with her.

'The whole thing caused a real shake-up at the school, the head got sacked over it all for *failing to provide a safe environment*, or something like that. Shame, he was a decent man, not sure what more he could have done; maybe he let the pupils have too much freedom, but that's what it was like in public schools in the '70s.

'The deputy head took over. He was a strange one. Never looked you in the eye; no idea where he is now, went abroad I think. She was also friendly with the gardener at Bentham, he's still there I think. He was an orphan like her, they were friends. He seemed harmless enough but you know they're usually the ones that end up as the serial killers in the films.'

He went back and sat in his armchair.

'Trouble was, we didn't have a body and no real evidence of any crime being committed, we couldn't make a case out of that. I always thought it was the deputy head or the PE teacher; if you believed the rumours they both had an eye for the young girls.'

'What about the gardener?'

'Kindred spirits. Both lost their parents at an early age. Both loved Bentham Woods and the Lake. I don't think he thought of Daisy in a sexual way; in fact I don't think he thought of anyone in that way. He loved his way of life, he didn't want for anything else, not jealous of anybody, great way to be really.'

'But was it all just an act?'

'If it was, I certainly didn't see through it.'

'Are any of the other suspects still local?' I sipped my tea and dunked another biscuit.

'Only the gardener I think. Most of the teachers would have moved on. It's going to be hellish difficult to pin this on anyone. Any evidence is long gone, unless you can try some of those DNA techniques on the bones or holdall?'

'Not a chance after all that time in the water. We may have found her, and we may have ruled out running away, and suicide, but I fear we're no closer to finding who murdered Daisy.'

'It will be worth you interviewing the gardener again. You might be able to break him, he's forty years older now.'

'I'll go and question him in the morning. It will be good to leave him to worry about it all night long. I'll get a couple of the boys to watch his cottage tonight, just in case he tries to leave.'

LOUISE

Sunday, September 9th, 1984

Louise gazed absent-mindedly out of her open bedroom window, across the landscaped grounds of Monkswood School. To the right, the avenue of Lombardy poplars flanked the drive up to the school. To the left, between their cottage and the school itself, were two great cedars of Lebanon, standing majestic, just as they would have done for the last two centuries. One on either side of the driveway. Perfect symmetry everywhere. As if her husband had designed it all himself.

Louise smiled, enjoying the warming rays of the early autumnal sun on her face. The Michigan countryside around her old home was beautiful, but rural Gloucestershire on a warm, cloudless September day took some beating. She knew she had landed on her feet. She pondered fate for a few moments, how things could have been so different. If her first husband had not cheated on her, she would probably still be a teacher in Lowell, Kent County, in the state of Michigan. She would never have travelled to England, never applied for the position of PE Teacher at Monkswood. And most importantly, never have met Matthew.

Louise was dragged back into the present by a movement in their garden below. It was Matthew. The high winds of yesterday had brought down the first conkers of the season. Louise watched as he carefully picked up the glossy brown conkers and put them into his pocket. Then he swept up the green prickly outer cases; even from her bedroom window she could see their white insides, a white as pure as freshly fallen snow.

Louise smiled again, who else would bother? Only Matthew, but then Matthew really loved his school. He always wanted it to look perfect. Especially today, when the pupils would be returning for the new school year. She wondered what the new school year would bring.

LAWRENCE

Monday, September 10th, 1984
Lawrence was always up early, but this morning he was ready even earlier than usual. Kate, his ex-wife, would be dropping their daughter Emma off. It was the first day of the new term, and no one wanted to be late first day back.

He sat at the picnic bench in his back garden and sipped his tea, enjoying the peace and quiet. He wondered what the morning would have been like had he still been living with Kate and Emma. He imagined raised voices, frayed tempers, as everyone tried to get ready on time. Kate would have needed to be out first, maybe before seven, running an audit at some godforsaken company miles away. He would be the one getting Emma's breakfast. Now, since the divorce, all he had to do was run Emma to school, collect her afterwards and give her some dinner in the evening, before Kate picked her up around seven-thirty. Life was simpler now, but lonelier.

Lawrence got up and walked out of the back door. He looked down the track that ran through the woods to his cottage. No sign of Kate's car yet. In the clear blue sky above, Lawrence heard rapid, high-pitched chattering and looked up as five swallows flew over. They swooped in low over the stream at the bottom of the garden. He watched them as they joyfully skimmed the water. Were they just taking a drink or feeding on some hatching insects? Maybe they were stocking up for the long migration ahead. They lived in two places, a bit like Emma, but swallows didn't have any choice, there was no food for them here in the winter. At least Emma didn't have to fly ten thousand miles twice a year – Kate only lived four miles away.

He looked at his watch, Kate was cutting it fine, and then he heard the throaty roar of her Audi, as it travelled rather too quickly along the lane. He got up to meet them. The car braked quickly, its tyres working hard to grip on the gravel track. Emma got out, Kate didn't. She lowered the window.

'Sorry Lawrence, one of those mornings. Last week of the audit. I worked most of the weekend. I'm supposed to be in Swindon by eight. Now Emma, are you sure you have everything?'

'Yes, Mum,' she said without looking back.

'Drive safely, Kate,' but as Lawrence was saying this, Kate's window was already closing and she had started reversing out.

Emma gave her dad a hug.

'Sometimes I'm just so glad to get here, everything with Mum is at two hundred miles an hour. She just winds me up.'

'She means well, her job just gets to her sometimes. We'd better go.'

'OK, but let's drive slowly and wind the windows down, I need fresh air to calm down.'

As they drove the short distance to school, Lawrence smiled. Emma was a lot like him, which he knew also wound up Kate.

'What did you get up to this weekend?' he asked.

'Not much. Stayed with Gran most of it. With Mum working.'

'You could have helped me out at the bookshop on Saturday, it was pretty quiet, just a few parents picking up school books, but not much else. I'd have loved your company.'

'You know what Mum's like sometimes, doesn't want me spending even more time with you.'

Lawrence understood. Kate had told him often enough. She provided all the money to send Emma to Monkswood. She had provided all the money in the divorce settlement to keep his bookshop afloat and yet she was the one who had no life at all.

'Anyway, it will be nice for you to see all your friends again.'

'Do you know, I'm actually looking forward to school,' and with that Emma waved her left hand out of the car window. 'That looks like April's car. Yes, I can see Lucy and Max.'

Lawrence had already noticed. They followed them up the leafy drive of Monkswood and parked next to them. The kids jumped out and headed over to the school, leaving Lawrence and April staring after them.

'Do you remember when we felt like that?' April said. 'Where's the excitement for us? All we get to do now is provide a taxi service to this musty old wreck.'

'You don't mean it. It's got to be better than Corinium Comp,' replied Lawrence.

'We survived it, but I suppose you're right. Times have changed. Our Lucy would be expecting her second by now and they would all be experts at graffiti, drugs and burglary.'

'I've missed you, April,' Lawrence smiled.

'What, my charismatic personality, or my great looks? Or both?'

His smile widened and he felt an inner warmth, as he stared down at what he considered to be five feet seven inches of female perfection.

'Don't go all gooey on me,' she said. 'We've been through this before. It wouldn't work. I need shoes, handbags, clothes. You would need to sell more books in a day than you do now in a whole year. No, unless I change my shopping habits, I will have to stay married to that rich, selfish bastard of a husband of mine.'

He laughed. 'You're right, as usual. Anyway, how about a pot of tea? I don't have to open the shop until ten. We need to catch up, I haven't seen you since the end of June and I want to see your topless holiday snaps.'

'You're on. As long as I can see yours. Polly's, in ten.'

Stephen Collier lives in Northamptonshire. He was a police officer for thirty years and on retirement from the force wrote his debut novel, *Blind Murder*. Stephen runs his own internationally renowned police training consultancy here and in Hong Kong.

steve.collier@me.com

Kill Switch

1

Hong Kong, August 15th

Standing.

That's all anyone could do – stand. Within minutes you might as well have been standing in the shower with your clothes on. In the forty degree heat and rampant humidity of Hong Kong's hottest summer on record, Detective Inspector of Police, Mandy Lee, was standing.

Standing.

On the edge of the parade square outside the Hong Kong Police College junior officers' canteen.

Standing.

By her Toyota Prius CID car, wanting to get in and switch on the air con. To feel the cooling breeze around her. To dry her clinging white blouse.

Standing.

But it would be considered disrespectful to get into the car before her boss, Detective Superintendent of Police, William Ho, returned.

Standing.

During the morning in front of raw recruits telling them about her role in the Hong Kong Police murder squad.

She was anxious, however, to get back to the real world of policing. She'd only done the job at the college as a favour to her senior colleague, Detective Senior Inspector of Police, Martin Cheung. And what did she know really? She was the latest recruit to the murder squad. A post she had applied for a number of times, but never successfully, until now.

Now she was a murder detective. Her elation at getting the job was short-lived. Her family had been disappointed about her choice of career, and her father could not understand her desire to work as a police officer. He hated it. She had never convinced him and doubted she ever could. A rift had developed between them that had not been resolved.

As she stood, leaning on the car, she shaded her eyes and watched her students sitting in the sun outside the canteen and recalled her time at the college. Joining as a junior inspector, a proud moment for her, with one star on her shoulder. She marched from class to class in her plain green fatigues. She was up with the sunrise to run up the hill behind the college, past the gun range. It all seemed long ago.

Lee was a great believer in Hong Kong's independence. But since the handover the new rulers had begun the slow inexorable creep of Chinese communist capitalism, making it clear that by 2047 Hong Kong would be unrecognisable as a former British colony. At least she was in agreement with her father on this subject. Staying British would surely have been a better way forward.

She removed a packet of handkerchiefs from the pocket of her jacket which she'd put on the back seat of her car. Removing a tissue from the packet she wiped the perspiration from her brow and glanced at her smartwatch wondering how much longer she would have to wait for Ho.

As she considered telephoning him, she saw him making his way towards her across the football pitch-sized parade ground. From this distance, she noticed for the first time that his gait reminded her of a waddling duck and a fat waddling duck at that. Ho would have her marched out of the department if he knew that such a thought had crossed her mind.

He had not been present at her lecture, something for which she was both grateful and disappointed. She wanted to show him what she was capable of, but she was also grateful that he would not be able to critique her knowledge or delivery in the car on the way back to headquarters.

Ho arrived out of breath, and apologised for keeping her waiting as he got into the car. Lee climbed into the driver's seat next to him and started the engine. The quiet hum of the electric motor and the lights on the dashboard display was all that indicated it was running. She drove away acknowledging some of her students who waved at her as she left.

The journey back to headquarters was done in silence. Her boss was, it would seem, preoccupied with his own thoughts.

—

Hong Kong Police headquarters is situated in the Wan Chai district, on Hong Kong island. It is a fifty-storey high, modern skyscraper overlooking Hong Kong Harbour and has a huge Hong Kong Police badge high on the wall. Driving into the underground car park she stopped, and Ho got out leaving her without a further word. She knew he had a reputation, that his silence was not to be thought of as rude. It was just the way he was.

In the large air-conditioned, open plan office in the west wing, and on the fourteenth floor of police headquarters, Lee made her way to her desk. From there she could look out over the harbour, and across the Convention Centre where they'd held the handover ceremony.

The office was deserted. Most of her colleagues had finished, but she was the duty officer for the whole of the weekend and she knew that the heat, the tourists and the local gangs were an explosive mixture. And there was a British Navy warship in the harbour for the weekend, so something was bound to happen. She could almost guarantee it.

Her mobile phone rang. She looked at who was calling, questioned herself and, declining the call, put the phone back on her desk. She sighed heavily, pushed her jet-black hair out of her face and rubbed her eyes. She was tired.

Sitting back in her chair she opened the top drawer of her desk and removed a chocolate bar that had been kept solid by the air con. She stared out of the window across the bay and, as she ate, watched the sun sink and the lights come on. She never got bored by the way Hong Kong Harbour lit up at night.

She heard the lift door open, and realised she had been dozing. Several detectives came into the office, laughing and joking. They acknowledged Lee as they did so. A detective sergeant walked over to her.

'You look a bit lonely sitting there, Inspector,' he said in Cantonese. 'We're all going into Central for dinner, you can come along if you want?'

'Thanks, you go, I'll sort myself out. I'm on duty all weekend so I wouldn't be much company anyway.'

'OK,' the sergeant gave Lee a mock salute and sauntered back towards his colleagues at the other end of the office.

Lee thought about his invitation after they had left. She should have gone with them, but she really couldn't pretend to be sociable. In the meantime she decided to go home.

The humid night made it difficult to sleep. Her air con unit had packed up days ago and she was still waiting for maintenance to come and fix it. Her apartment, away from the hustle and bustle of the city, was of a moderate size; one bedroom, a kitchen and separate living room. It was economically furnished in a traditional Hong Kong style, a lot of red – for good luck. Her double-sized bed was the only concession to space in her bedroom. And she bought it simply because she knew that when she did get to sleep, it needed to be comfortable.

It didn't help though that the air con was bust, so the sticky night was spent drifting in and out of light sleep. At one point she removed her night clothes and just lay naked on the bed. She was almost relieved when she received a call at 5:24 am from her colleague, Cheung. Born and bred in Hong Kong, they both spoke in perfect English with each other, switching easily between colloquial Cantonese and English.

'What's up?'

'We've got a sus death in Lockhart Road, I need you here.'

'OK, where exactly?'

'You'll see, you can't miss us. I'm here already, I'll wait for you,' he ended the call.

Lee had a quick, cool shower and got dressed. Leaving her apartment she picked up the early MTR into Admiralty station. The underground line was quiet and she had the carriage to herself. She went into headquarters and collected a pool car before driving to Lockhart Road, though she could have walked. The area of Lockhart Road was only two blocks from headquarters.

Lee knew the area well. It had an array of pubs, styled in the same manner as those back in England, designed to make the ex-pats feel at home – or so she'd been told, never having managed to get over to the UK. There was also a mixture of pole dancing bars and nightclubs, some more seedy than others. And she knew there was a much darker side, a part of the city catering for the intimate desires of the single man or woman. Lee grew up knowing that prostitution was legal – with her slim physique and natural beauty, she came very close to being forced into that business herself. But these clubs all got plenty of business, particularly when an allied navy visited – quite enough to cause plenty of trouble.

Despite the hour, people and red urban taxis were milling around. A mixture of tourists and business people were being chucked out of the clubs, some of which were open twenty-four hours.

The club where Lee was going was one of those clubs. As she approached she saw several police vans, the Scientific Evidence van and Cheung's battered old Datsun sitting on the corner, by the steak house.

The police activity had already caused a great deal of interest. Cheung stood outside the club, a cigarette hanging out of his mouth. He had both hands stuffed in the pockets of his white linen suit. She could see, even from a distance, that there were patches of sweat under his arms. She swiftly checked her own as she parked opposite the club, then walked across the road.

'What do we have then, Inspector?' she asked as she approached him.

'Hooker dead upstairs,' he indicated in the general direction of inside with a movement of his thumb, then put his hand back in his pocket.

'Have you been up?'

'Briefly,' his voice was flat.

'Seen the body?'

He nodded.

'Anyone up there now?'

'Got a uniform on the door, SEOs waiting till we've done our preliminaries.' Cheung's gaze wandered around the area of the street in front of him, seemingly indifferent to the reason as to why they were there.

'Doctor?' Lee asked.

'No, told me he'd examine the body at the morgue.'

'He's not coming out then?' Lee asked.

Cheung shook his head.

'Shall we go up?'

Cheung shrugged.

'Well, that's what we're here for, isn't it?'

'I suppose.'

Lee looked at Cheung. Although she'd only been working with him for the six months she'd been on the unit, she had seen a distinct change in him. He looked constantly tired, sometimes withdrawn, with that ever present cigarette.

She had never been able to get from him why he was so dispirited all the time. Perhaps, when she got to know him better, he might take her into his confidence. But she knew that she wouldn't have been partnered with him if he weren't good at his job.

2

They both entered the club through the black heavy curtains that covered the entrance – a feeble attempt to prevent those passing who might be of a naïve disposition from seeing what was going on inside.

They moved from the early dawn into almost pitch darkness. Despite what had happened the owner had evidently not considered putting on the lights and sending all his other punters home. He was standing behind his bar. Cheung strode up to him as he chatted to a young girl sitting on a stool in a sparkly gold micro-dress. Cheung didn't take any notice of her, but spoke fast and loud to the owner.

'Why have you not closed this bar as instructed?'

'It costs me money if I close!'

'I don't care, this is a murder scene, and you *will* close.'

'What about my girls?'

'They stay here now until we have interviewed them.'

'While I'm not working, I don't get paid,' the girl on the stool said to them both.

'That's not my problem, but everyone will be interviewed before they leave. Do you understand?' Cheung pointed at the owner.

The bar owner said nothing and, with some reluctance, skulked away and did what he was told. 'Shall we go up then?' Cheung called to Lee half-heartedly.

Lee nodded and they made their way to the stairs, situated to the left of the bar, and passed through a curtained doorway. They reminded Lee of a set of curtains which she had seen in her local restaurant being made of plastic multicoloured strips interspersed with plastic crystals. They jangled as they pushed them aside.

Behind the doorway, at the bottom of the stairs, was a reception desk. There was no one sitting behind it now. The owner had tried to make the reception area respectable, but to Lee it was just cheap. The stairs were covered with a red carpet with yellow dragon motifs and the walls were painted black. At the top of the stairs a hallway extended the length of premises.

She could see that halfway down the hall was a uniformed branch officer, standing guard at a black-painted door. Cheung and Lee walked towards the officer who acknowledged them as they prepared to enter. Lee removed latex gloves and a mask from a personal protection pouch she had on her belt next to her gun holster. She put on a pair of overshoes, handed to her by the officer on the door from a box at his feet, snapped on her gloves and attached her mask before entering the room. Cheung did the same thing, but appeared far more lazy about it.

Cheung stood on the threshold of the door. Lee stood slightly behind and to the right of him so she could also see inside. He moved directly into the corner of the room where an air conditioning unit was pumping out cold air. It squeaked and a metallic grinding sound made its operation very loud.

Lee looked towards the body of a woman on the bed.

'Pretty girl,' Cheung commented.

Lee said nothing as she continued to survey the girl and her surroundings before taking a step closer. Cheung let her take the lead.

'Tell me what you see,' he said.

'A female, lying on her back, on the left-hand side of a large double bed with black silk bed sheets. Her right leg and right arm hanging over the side, her head turned to the right. Blue eyes open, with no obvious signs of life. She's wearing a silk housecoat that's fallen open. She's white, naked.'

Cheung remained silent.

'Across her abdomen there appear to be numerous stab wounds. And yet there is little blood here.'

She looked towards Cheung. He still stood in front of the air con unit.

'I can't understand why there is so little blood, with all these stab wounds, Inspector?'

Cheung took a step forward and bent down to look under the bed by the side on which she lay.

'There's not a lot of blood underneath her either, not on the floor or under the bed.'

'She wasn't done here then?' Lee said.

Cheung concurred, bobbed his head and took a step back, closer again to the air con unit. He'd lit another cigarette, and put it in its usual position, hanging out of the side of his mouth. He removed a small screw-top jar from his pocket, into which he dropped ash from his cigarette. Lee wondered whether he was even interested in solving the crime. The stories about his investigative techniques were well known around the force. He was meticulous in his quest for the truth, catching the perpetrator and seeing that the victim's family received the justice they needed.

Now, standing in front of the air con unit, he certainly didn't look as if he wanted to solve anything. And that bloody cigarette. She knew he was aware that it could compromise everything if it ever got to court, screw-top jar or not, but it was not her position to tell him that which he already knew.

Lee returned to the task in hand, but she was even more convinced that Cheung was becoming a liability when dealing with such human detritus. He'd been alluding to it for months.

Hong Kong murder detectives were used to coming to these places to clear up the mess of local triads, drug dealers and sex slave cartels trying to muscle in on each other's patch. But working with someone who even regarded himself as a liability was a concern she could not ignore for much longer. Surely Superintendent Ho had noticed.

Putting those thoughts to the back of her mind, Lee could not help but think that Cheung might be right, that this girl was just another hooker. Weren't they always in this part of town? But as she surveyed the scene she was beginning to realise that something was not quite right. Lee moved closer to the body.

'Would you like to hazard a guess at what you think has gone on here? Your interpretation of the scene is, as far as I can see, correct,' Cheung said suddenly. 'Let me have your initial impressions.'

Lee watched Cheung remove the cigarette from his mouth and hold it in his right hand, tapping ash into his jar, but he still didn't move from the air con.

'Well, she's not Filipino, that's for sure,' Lee said.

Cheung nodded and took another pull on his cigarette.

'As I said, I don't think she was killed here, unless these wounds,' she indicated to the woman's stomach, 'were administered post-mortem.'

She walked around the bed. There was a bedside table on each side of the bed. The one closest to the body had had its contents strewn over the floor. Lee wondered whether this was as the result of the act of murder or whether it happened when the body was deposited on the bed. She became more and more convinced that this scene was a set-up. Certain things were out of place.

'There are none of the victim's street clothes here. No personal belongings, no handbag.'

Lee moved around the room in search of personal belongings – nothing.

She needed to record her thoughts. She looked at her watch.

'Do you need to be somewhere?' Cheung asked.

She smiled at Cheung 'No, just making a few notes.'

He raised an eyebrow.

'On my phone,' she confirmed.

'You look like Dick Tracy.'

'Who?'

'You wouldn't know him – too young. Continue,' Cheung said, waving an arm unenthusiastically.

'You'll have to tell me who he is later then,' she smiled and invoked the audio notebook on her watch and started recording what she knew and continued.

'There appears to be bruising at the top of her legs and a small amount of blood around her genitals,' she stopped again and looked down the victim's legs. 'Her toes are painted blue as are her fingernails, well manicured. No evidence of scratching or anything under the nails that may help the investigation at this time. No nails are broken. Her left arm is by her side, with the wrist and hand underneath her left buttock. Her right arm has fallen over the side of the bed,' she paused and felt Cheung standing beside her, 'do you know how long she could have been here?'

'Impossible to say in this place,' he said, 'people come and go like the wind. It's possible she was brought up here already dead. We'd have to ask the owner.'

'Have we started those enquiries?'

'Yes, the uniform branch are talking to the staff and other employees now.'

'Let's hope they come up with something.'

'What else do you notice, Inspector?'

Lee glanced around the room. The items that had been knocked off the bedside table weren't out of the ordinary, just a lamp and an ashtray. Looking across at the other table on the opposite side of the bed to where the woman lay, nothing on this table appeared to have been disturbed, in fact it seemed too... *right*. She continued talking into her watch as she walked towards the table.

'Two cocktail glasses and an opened condom wrapper. The rubber is still inside, unused. It'll be interesting to see what the autopsy shows. If she's been raped or otherwise sexually assaulted we might be able to get some DNA.'

'Assuming the rapist did kill her and assuming that she didn't have consensual sex,' interrupted Cheung.

'It must have been rough sex to cause the bruising to her legs.'

'I've seen worse.'

Lee raised an eyebrow and continued. 'The glasses look as if they've had some blue liquid in,' she sniffed one of the glasses, 'Gin, curaçao, probably a Corpse Reviver.'

'How do you know that?'

'You should get out more, Inspector.'

For the first time since they arrived, Cheung smiled at Lee's comment. She waited for more of a response, but it didn't come.

Lee went back and stood at the end of the bed, searching the woman with a calculating eye.

'These wounds to the stomach,' she said at last, 'definitely a blade of some sort but they look strange.'

'What do you mean?'

'They don't appear to have been inflicted with the violence that one would normally expect. There's normally some tearing around the wound. These wounds seem almost... surgical,' Lee removed her smart phone from the inside pocket of her jacket, and tapped for an app. She took a photo close-up of each of the wounds, then invoked an app that looked like a magnifying glass. She looked closely at the wounds, and beckoned Cheung over.

'I prefer my own,' he responded to Lee's beckoning. He removed an ancient magnifying glass from his pocket. Lee smiled. The old and the new, she thought. They held their glasses over the wounds

'I see what you mean,' Cheung said, 'what don't you see, Inspector?'

'I don't see any marks where the hilt of the knife connected to the body. Even if she'd only been here a couple of hours, she would still show some bruising, surely?'

'I agree, but perhaps it'll be more obvious in time.'

'We need to ensure that the forensic pathologist takes a close look during his examination.'

'Well, let's hope we get some answers to that later.'

'I know we don't know who she is, but are we going to make an assumption that at this time she's a hooker?'

'We can ask the owner as to whether she's a regular?'

'We'll do that before we leave.'

Lee saw that Cheung was becoming more animated now, looking around the room. Perhaps the thoughts that had preoccupied him were now at the back of his mind. But Lee was still concerned about his lack of enthusiasm.

'Does she look like a hooker to you?' Cheung asked.

'What do you think a hooker looks like?'

Cheung shrugged. 'Well, they're not normally this healthy, are they?'

'Tourist possibly – trying her luck. It has been known.'

Chueng's mouth turned down in a gesture of not knowing and he looked back at the woman. Lee noticed him staring.

'Inspector?' she asked. 'What?'

'I was thinking, she's obviously been out in the sun, there are distinct tan marks from a bikini. She's sunbathed here, or elsewhere. She's well-manicured, not unattractive, there are none of her clothes in the room other than what she's wearing. She just doesn't seem the type to end her life up here in this fleapit of a club in Lockhart Road,' Cheung thought for a moment, 'perhaps we need to start with the hotels. See if anyone has not been back to their room, or not taken a room that they'd booked. Perhaps also we need to compare her face to the immigration database to see if any faces match hers. Get the mortuary photos of her over to Immigration first off.'

Lee nodded. Cheung moved towards the door, and called the Scientific Evidence Officers back into the room. He nodded to Lee and without a further word he left.

Kate Simants worked for several years as a TV journalist, specialising in undercover reporting. Her novel *Lock Me In* was shortlisted for the CWA Debut Dagger, and she received the UEA Literary Festival Scholarship for the Crime Fiction MA. A keen roller derby player, Kate lives near Bristol with her family.

katesimants@hotmail.com

The Knocks

Night. Real, dense, outdoors night, nothing like the safe, half-lit gloom he's known from a life in the city. Here, the trees all around hold the darkness tight, pressing it in. Behind him, the distant thrum of the M5, but so low and constant that it's just a layer under the silence, like silt. Apart from that, nothing. Just the thud and scrape of his spade striking the earth, pulling loose, striking again.

There's a ghost of rain, breathable, invisible. Cold and so fine it might as well be dust, sticking to whatever it touches. But the boy is anything but cool, because digging is hard, hard work. Has he even done it before, ever? At his old house. He thinks of the garden as he brings the spade down. The flowers. They spread and bloom in his mind, and he colours them in reds and purples and blues and the world is made vivid again. His mum grew them, so he must have helped. He must have gardened.

But that's not the same as this, here. Gardening is for growing things. This is something else.

The spade is starting to grind now that he's getting further down. The top layer was easy: twigs and leaves and mulch all softened from the winter above and the rot below. Now, waist-deep, it's getting stony. He stops, breathing hard. He lets the long handle fall against the side of the pit – he'll call it a pit, because that's as far as he can let this go, in his head. He pushes his fists into his spine, gets his breath back. Listening, watchful, although he's been here enough times to know how rare visitors are. Without passing by boat on the water that's just through there, only a few feet away, it would be hard to know the clearing was here at all. He turns to watch the river, immense and silent, sliding blindly west towards Bristol, and then Portishead, and then the sea. He thinks of the thing they did at school about the water table, too. He digs any deeper, any minute now he's going to hit it.

His pit isn't as deep as he wanted, but it'll have to do. He turns to tell the man, but he has to scan the blackness for a moment until he spots him, crouching, at the edge of the clearing. Head in his hands. Could be crying. The boy doesn't care.

He climbs out of the pit. Right at the edge, there's the girl. Lying on her side exactly where he set her down. Facing him.

He wipes his forehead with the back of his sleeve. Considering the size of her, considering how he could probably circle her waist with his hands, getting her there from the car they parked maybe half a mile away was like carrying a sack of rocks. Dead weight: that's what it's called. He had to keep shifting the load, her stomach folded across his shoulder. Closer to her than he'd ever dreamed, his hand splayed across the back of her thigh, just to hold her steady in the fireman's lift. The man could have done it but the boy wouldn't let him. This was the deal. He'd do whatever the man told him to afterwards, but they did this part *his* way.

He closes his eyes now and runs it back, cementing the feel of her in his memory. The swish of her hair, hanging down behind him, thick enough to feel it brush against his jeans. He runs over the sensations of it, the bounce of her hands against the backs of his knees. Could he feel the contours of her chest, upside down, against his shoulder blades? Yes. He tells himself the feel of it is a memory, not imagined. He *could* feel that. And the warmth of her skin, even through the clothes? Yes.

The beating of her heart?

He opens his eyes. Swallows hard.

Yes. He remembers that too. He wants it badly enough, so he takes the blank and fills it with the detail and then it's there, in his version of it, for good. He remembers it all.

Half-covered with the battered tarp, she is motionless. The tips of his fingers sing with the desire to reach out and touch her. They ache with it. The drizzle has sunk into her hair, binding the strands into damp cords; it's settled into a sheen on her face, catching scraps of light that skitter across the ground as the canopy of leaves shifts above her. Her eyes are closed. Her checked shirt clings in sodden folds around her motionless body. And she is beautiful.

She is *beautiful*.

He forces himself to look away and he calls over to the man in a low voice.

'Ready.'

It's not a question. It's a command. He is in charge.

The man says, 'Right,' and he stands, like he's a hundred years old, like it's the hardest thing he's ever had to do. He comes closer, and his arms are folded. He comes right up to where she's lying but he doesn't touch her.

'Anyone finds it, it's on you.'

'I know,' the boy says.

'I still think we should burn it.'

The boy shakes his head, but the man is eyeing him. Wants convincing. So the boy says, 'The rain. Too damp for it. And even if we could, the smoke. Smell. Not worth the risk. This way is better.'

The man pushes the shape under the tarp with the toe of his shoe. 'Let's get it done then.'

'No!' The boy's shout is thin and high with panic, and the man snaps round and his eyes shine silver in the darkness and he puts his hands up, surrendering.

'Jesus. What?'

'Don't touch her,' the boy says. Spits it. 'Don't even fucking *touch* her.' And it's all he can do not to drive him into the pit instead of her. Grab the spade and swing the edge against the side of his head. But he doesn't do it. He made a promise.

Because she is his. Eight months he's loved her, and tonight he's done something for her that no one else could do, and no one else will ever know, and he will do every part of it himself, and that means she's his. It makes her *his*. He breathes hard, staring at the man. Teeth tight. He could kill him. He could.

'Do it then,' the man says, stepping back. 'Go on.'

And the boy does. He sits at the edge of the pit like he's getting into a pool, and he lowers himself down. Gets his hands underneath her armpits, careful to keep as much of her covered with the tarp as he can. He starts to pull. At first she doesn't move, and then there's the sound of a tear, fabric and *oh God* he hopes he hasn't hurt her. He winces, but he keeps pulling, and all of a sudden the resistance is gone and she pitches in, shoulders hitting him awkwardly against the fronts of his thighs, and he staggers back, recovers, and lowers her down. Softly. Soundless.

He moves her so she's lying on her side, her back to the man, and he starts to cover her again, as gently as breathing, with the tarp. He takes one last look at her before he lowers it: the smears of black under her eyes, the tiny silver star at her neck on a chain so fine you almost don't see it. And then he starts to climb out.

Until the man says, 'Hold on.'

'What?'

From his pocket the man brings out a flick knife. He tosses it down, and the boy catches it.

The man, half-turned away, nods towards her. 'Clothes.'

The boy's heart stops still.

'Her clothes,' the man says again. 'They'll have fibres on them. Both of us – our hair, on her clothes. Particles. You want them finding that?'

The boy says nothing. The knife is impossibly heavy in his hand.

'Cut them off,' the man tells him. 'We're going to burn them. And ours, make sure.'

He looks down at her. The rain is still falling, little puddles forming, black like oil.

He can't take her clothes. He can't leave her in a pit, naked.

'Now,' the man says. 'Or the deal's off.'

So the boy doesn't have any choice. His heart convulsing in his throat, he kneels.

'Don't look,' he tells the man.

'What?'

'I said don't look. You don't get to look at her.'

The man shakes his head at him with pure hatred. But he does what he's told and turns his back.

The boy puts the knife in his back pocket, folds the tarp off, and rolls her onto her back. Her hair spreads like a wing over her face. He unbuttons her jeans, lifts her hips, and pulls, whispering, 'I'm sorry, I'm sorry,' so quietly he can hardly hear it over the tapping of the rain on the tarp. He won't look at her.

A bird screams overhead.

'Get the fuck on with it,' the man says over his shoulder.

Through barely-open eyes, the boy finishes the job, but he doesn't use the knife. He does it tenderly, without lingering. All of it: shirt, socks, the rest. He piles the clothes beside him, covers her over again.

'Done.'

'Necklace,' the man says. He's turned around.

'I *said* don't look—'

'*Necklace*,' the man says again, snarling now.

The boy does as he's told. And when it's done, her hair catches around his fingers. As he unwinds it, careful not to uproot a single thread, he thinks of something else.

He looks up. 'Her hair.'

'What about it?'

The boy blinks against the intensifying rain. 'You said. Fibres. There'll be my hair in hers, probably.' He doesn't know if that's how it works, but the idea is taking hold now. He has to convince him. 'And yours. If they can find fibres in her clothes, I mean, why not in her hair? Not worth the risk.'

The man flinches, nods. 'Cut it then. Close as you can. Wrap it in the clothes, we'll burn it all later.'

The boy grunts, and flips open the knife, and this time he doesn't waste a moment.

He doesn't know it yet, but what he's doing now, it's going to be the cage around every dream he'll have for the rest of his life. And every one of those dreams, from which he'll wake as if someone has forced an icy fist down through his mouth and taken hold of his heart, will end the same.

An image of the girl he loved harder than anyone, the girl he would have given his life for, if she would have only let him do it, if it might have made her love him back:

Her skin, white as bone, streaked with earth and rain.

The last filaments of her hair falling from her scalp as she stands, naked, her arms loose against the sides of her flawless, living, perfect body. Her nipples tight and her belly smooth and her legs solid and strong.

Her smile as she comes closer and closer until her face is against his.

And her breath in his ear, and her voice, as soft as a blanket of snow.

'*Thank you. Thank you.*'

1

HMP Bristol

February 27th, 2016

Wren Reynolds pulled into the designated *Probation Service* bay, put the engine out of its misery, and huffed at her hands. Almost March, but cold as midwinter. To her right, long wet stretches of overnight rain had darkened the concrete under the windows of B-Wing. Behind it, a flat, colourless sky.

On the passenger seat, she found the printout of the room booking. CB009, Community Building. The newest addition to the complex, tucked behind the original red-brick Victorian edifice and clad, inexplicably, in dusky pink weatherboard. Cold clean air flooded the car as she opened the door. The day was brisk and bright. It was the kind of morning a person might hope for, if they were planning a fresh start.

Her offender had six days left inside. He was, numerically, still a young man. The details of his face floated to the front of her mind as she stood, pushing off the trainers she wore for driving and slipping on her work shoes. She blinked, forcing him away, but he resurfaced. He always resurfaced.

The mental image she had of him was out of date. He could be skinnier or fatter by now, or bulked up with weights and chin-ups the way they sometimes did. One thing she knew: inmates did not come out the same as they went in, not if they served as long as he had. Three years and ten months. Average stay in Bristol was seven months. He was twenty-one years old but he'd be the grandfather of B-Wing, part of the bolted-down furniture. She recalled the heavy forehead and the dark, blank glare. Impenetrable, near-black eyes a person could trip into and never hit the bottom.

Ashworth.

Robert Malachy Ashworth.

She straightened her new skirt – grey wool, magenta pinstripes, a flash of turquoise lining at the back to match the tights – then reached back into the car to get her things: handbag, phone, files. Props. Things she held on to, to tell her who she was meant to be.

He was just an offender, just the person she had been assigned. He would not know her.

She eased her three-quid coffee from the cup-holder before bumping the door shut with her hip. The alarm beeped as she walked away, locking the car automatically, and her shoes clacked on the tarmac, sending a report across the still empty car park. Beyond the buildings, an amplified voice ordered prisoners around in the yard, the sound of it cutting through the drone of the M32 to the east. The place was only just coming to life, and Wren was deliberately early. He was still theirs, but on the cusp of probation. This was the overlap of past and future, of incarceration and what came next.

The reception doors slid open and she lifted the lanyard round her neck to show the ID card hanging from it. The woman behind the acrylic window leaned closer, and pushed her glasses up her nose.

'Community Atonement Programme,' she read slowly, then turned her suspicious gaze up to Wren's face before softening in recognition. 'Oh right. It's you. What do you do now, then?

'Same as ever,' she said, shrugging. 'Whisk them away for a new life, free from crime.'

The two women deadpanned that together for a moment, then broke at the same time and laughed.

'It's still probation,' Wren said, looping the card off her neck and sliding it into the metal tray. 'It's the accelerated release thing. CAP.' She took a mouthful of coffee as the receptionist, her face pinched with the effort of dredging her memory, shook her head.

Wren swallowed. 'It's been on the news?'

'Don't watch the news.' Holding up an apologetic, *one minute* finger, the receptionist disappeared with the ID into a side room.

Wren leaned against the counter and waited. It was the first day of her new job. Probation and Rehabilitation Professional, as distinct from the full Probation Officer role she'd had for the last year. As a bona fide former PO, Wren was overqualified, and had expected questions asked about why she chose to take the pay cut. But the management knew a good deal when they saw it and had said nothing.

In the five-city experiment, a total of 104 offenders would be released between six and twenty-four months early. *Carefully screened offenders –* according to the CAP press release – *will make contact with those people most affected by his or her criminal actions, in order to understand and apologise for the repercussions of the crime.* Scrape away the jargon and the gilding and what was left was an emergency valve to release the pressure on the UK's critically overpopulated prisons. Make them say sorry nicely, and let them out early. Known briefly in the tabloid press as the Lout's Lottery.

Known to the people like Wren as The Knocks.

The woman returned. 'So you're still National Probation Service?'

'Yep.'

'But just more optimistic.' She tented her fingers under her chin, pleased with her joke.

Wren pointed and winked. 'You got it.'

'Proper job.' She slid the ID and a plastic keycard through on the tray.

'All the way to the back, double doors, and follow it to the right.'

Wren thanked her and followed the directions. Breakfast would only just have been over but the place was already dense with the high-volume catering smells of £1.27-or-less lunches: onions, meat, potato reconstituted from pellets. She mouth-breathed, keeping it shallow, until she exited the wide central thoroughfare and emerged into the Community Building.

The mechanism on the door received her card, whirred for a moment, then gave her a green light. She stepped inside. The room was overheated and smelled of new paint. There were two access doors – the one for visitors, and another on the opposite wall which, when unlocked, opened into B-Wing. Three of the walls were regulation grey; the fourth matched the garish exterior.

Wren went to open a window, the heel of her shoe catching briefly in the flooring. She almost smiled. *Carpet*, she thought. *Heating*. She could practically feel the prison's Victorian founders turning in their graves. She sipped her coffee and went to open a window that looked out onto the rec yard.

Beyond, there was a view, grand and unbroken thanks to the prison's elevation. Sited on the crest of Horfield, the main facility looked north, but the Community Building was afforded a broad, southerly sweep down to the best of Bristol, the postcard bits. Temple Meads; Suspension Bridge; St Mary Redcliffe; the blunt, unfinished-looking tower of the Wills Memorial; even the spiral car park of the new Cabot Circus shopping centre was imposing from up there in BS7. Two hundred years ago when the first bricks of the prison were laid, most of that historic skyline hadn't even been built. All the same, someone along the line had made the decision to construct the prison with its back to the city that had grown lawless enough to need it.

Or it could have been that Wren was overthinking it. That happened. She'd been waiting for this for a long time. There had been a lot of time to think.

An office-supply clock on the wall told her there were six minutes until the meeting. The prisoner would be on his way. She imagined him walking along the platform outside his cell, pausing every thirty feet for the warden to slide a new key in a new lock, marvelling at his luck being chosen for the new programme, recommended for accelerated release. Under the impression that release would be the end of all of it, the shame and the boredom and the godawful food. He'd be thinking that as long as he turned up to his appointments and kept his curfews, everything he'd done to get himself in there would be water under the bridge. And the people who'd been felled and broken and twisted into tight, bloody shreds by the grief he'd caused: all of those people might as well never have existed.

And maybe he'd have been right about some of that. But not all of it.

Just a few minutes, now. She clasped her hands together, turned them inside out and pushed until her lats creaked. If she was nervous, it was because the project was new. New protocols, interest from the press, brass with a point to prove, more at stake than just letting them out and keeping them out of trouble. That was all.

The chair spread slightly under her weight when she sat, and she crossed her legs to avoid the press of the armrests on the outside of her thighs. She smoothed her skirt across her lap, then unpacked: files, a single pen, notebook.

She was ready.

Voices in the corridor. She looked up: *his* voice. He'd said only a few dozen words during his hearing, but she wouldn't forget that voice. Not ever.

She touched her hair and reminded herself that she was unrecognisable. She wore make-up now, and her sleek, mid-length bob was so wildly different from the mousy crop of back then that no one would make the connection. No one. But the dark thing in her chest shifted and she found she was standing again.

A beep from the lock on the other side of the room, the prisoner's door. She stood, straightened. *Just another offender.* And he would not know her.

The door swung open.

'Miss Reynolds.' The warden was not one she knew. Tall, thin, borderline friendly.

Wren hadn't been *Miss* anything since she was seventeen but she didn't correct him. She nodded, and he stepped aside, and there he was.

Robert Malachy Ashworth, formerly of Isambard Court, Southmead. White, six-two. His dark hair was unchanged, cropped tight against his angular skull, but his narrow shoulders were rounded, like he was holding something in his belly. She wondered if it was remorse. She doubted it.

Wren put out a hand. He looked at it for a moment before turning his bottle-brown eyes to hers. In the few endless seconds he held her gaze, Wren's spine and everything close to it turned to ice. The slightest frown gathered on his forehead but she maintained the eye contact, held it like a talisman.

You don't know me. You do not know me.

In a soft baritone the warden said, 'This lady's your probation officer, Ashworth.'

'Right.'

He looked away, and she silently let out the breath she hadn't meant to hold.

'Shake the lady's hand, bud.'

Ashworth did as he was told, with the air of a man who did as he was told.

The skin of his palm was soft and warm against hers. An unpunished hand. Letting go, he passed his gaze down towards her throat, then straight to his shoes.

He told them he was pleased to meet her.

Wren gave the warden a nod. 'I can take it from here, thanks.'

'Buzzer's on the wall,' he said before he left. 'Hit it when you're finished.'

Then the door closed, and they were alone.

Somewhere in the building there was a short klaxon. Wren sat down, and invited Ashworth to do the same. He lifted his chair to angle himself away from the window, his shoulder to the view, and sat. Wren's heart was firing out ball bearings instead of blood.

She drank the remaining inch of cold coffee, slid the cup to the side.

'So,' she said. 'You're getting out. Congratulations.'

'Why am I, though?' he said in a voice dry with disuse. His face was set as hard as concrete.

'Community Atonement Programme,' she told him. 'It was in the letter. You get out early in exchange for a few visits to people affected by your crime. I'm going to take you round, and we're going to have some conversations. The idea is that you find out what your actions have done, long term. Understand the wider repercussions.'

'What people?' Not a blink. Maybe not concrete after all: something older. Volcanic rock, maybe.

She shrugged. 'There's a list. Victims of the crime. People connected to your accomplice.'

'Paige.'

The slightest twist of nausea, hearing her name in his voice. 'Yeah. Paige Garrett.'

'And by *victim*, you're saying I've got to talk to Yardley.' He leaned back in his chair, pressing his fingertips against his scalp.

'Yep. Being the man you burgled, kind of qualifies him as the victim. You cracked his head on a wall. And then there was his wife, if you remember.'

He said nothing.

'Do you know she's on four kinds of medication related to the trauma, Robert?'

'It's Rob.' He rubbed his fingertips slowly across his eyebrows. 'And no. I did not know that.'

'Well, *Rob*, she is.' She flipped open the file, making a big thing of finding the right page. 'First year after you broke into her home and tied her up, she lost her hair. Alopecia. Know about that?'

He grunted, muttered something she didn't catch. 'What was that?'

'I said, *I* didn't tie her up. Wasn't me.'

'Right.' She gave him a long look. Technically, it was true. 'I'm not alone in doubting that Paige would have thought of that herself, though.'

Paige Garrett had still been a child when he'd taken her on his romp around James Yardley's gated home. Fifteen, with a record that was not so much clean as immaculate. Non-existent. Which wouldn't have been such a big deal, but coupled with the fact that she'd spent the preceding eleven years in state care? It was more than a big deal. It was a miracle.

But it was for later, all of that.

'You're a lucky man, being selected,' she told him, uncapping a pen.

'Lucky. Yeah.' There could have been anything hiding behind those eyes.

She pulled the sheet of standard conditions from its plastic wallet and read them aloud: that he would report to her on a twice-weekly basis; that they would form a plan regarding his accommodation and return to work; that breaking any licence condition could mean recall to prison. *You will, you will not. If you do x, then y.* The state's last attempt at drilling in the causal nature of crime and punishment. He nodded at each clause, until she was done.

'And then there's the special conditions,' she said. 'For the programme.'

He looked up. Full attention.

She read him the list of names, the people they would be meeting. The victims, obviously. Paige's friends. Teachers.

'*Paige*'s teachers?'

'Yes.'

'Why? They didn't give a fuck. What difference would any of it make to *them*?'

Wren held his gaze. These were questions she'd had to push through in the office, and she'd got it down to a fine art. 'Because in the absence of family, we have to go a little further to find the people who loved her.'

'But I didn't do anything to her!'

'You did,' she said. Ashworth opened his mouth to complain but she held up a finger. 'You *did*. And you don't get to control what we do here. Understood?'

He gave her a long, flat look. 'Fine.'

She continued the list of visits: Paige's friends, the children's home where Paige lived – which had also been the home of Ashworth's younger brother, Luke. With every name, his stare slid lower until he was directing the full beam of it into the table, as if he was trying to set the thing on fire.

'Do I get to see Paige?'

She looked up slowly from the sheet. His eyes stayed locked on the space in front of him.

Robert Ashworth had been the last person to see her, before she disappeared. The private CCTV from Yardley's house on the night of the burglary showed him arguing with her before they broke into the house. Later, he'd fled the scene with no thought for her safety when the police arrived. He'd been found a few hours later. But Paige was never seen again.

'Do I?' he repeated.

Wren had been sure, had been absolutely certain, that he was the one person who would know if she was alive or dead.

'You tell me,' she said. She watched for a flinch, a flick of the eyes. A tell. But nothing came. 'Do *you* know where she is?'

'No.'

'No?'

'No.'

But then she saw it, a glint of it escaping before he managed to get it locked down.

Fear.

Of what?

You wanted him to rot, she told herself. She wanted him to rot, and he failed to rot. And now he was here.

There were forms that needed signing. She slid them across the table, and he took them, took the pen, filled them out, slid them back wordlessly.

When they were finished with the paperwork, she rang the buzzer and almost immediately footsteps sounded in the corridor again.

The heavy door swung open and the warden stepped into the room.

'All done?'

'Pretty much, for now,' she said. She gestured to Ashworth that he could stand, that they were finished, but he didn't move.

He nodded, infinitesimally, at the space in front of her. 'Is Luke on your list?'

'Your brother?'

Another nod. 'Haven't seen him since I got here.'

Luke Ashworth, thirteen at the time, making him sixteen, seventeen now. Friend of Paige Garrick. Clean record. Questioned on three occasions by the police about the events leading up to her disappearance. The transcripts read like a séance: lots and lots in the way of questions, very little in the way of anything else. You'd be forgiven for thinking the brothers had planned their silence in advance.

'He's not on the list, no. But there's no restriction on you getting in touch with him,' she said, tidying her gear away. The warden ushered Ashworth out of his seat and towards the door.

'Luke might know where she is,' he said, eyes hard on Wren's. 'Because I sure as hell don't.'

You wanted him to rot.

'Ashworth,' warned the screw. 'Now.'

Ashworth waited, resisting the pull of the hand on his thick bicep.

'We'll see,' she told him, like it was nothing much to her. 'Plenty of time.'

Something like life flickered for a moment around his eyes before he remembered where he was, and crushed it. The warden jerked suddenly sideways as Ashworth released his counterbalance and moved as bidden into the corridor. He gave her one last look before the four-inch-thick door swung closed.

She meant what she said. They had plenty of time. They had as long as it took.

MARIE OGÉE

Marie Ogée is a lecturer in English by day and tries to be a writer at night. She lives in Bordeaux when she has to work but her house in Dordogne is where she gets most of her writing done. For some odd reason, she likes to write in airports too.

ogee.marie@orange.fr

Noir

1—*Fuck you ladies*

Michel Lefort was a good guy. He had been a good boy first and then a good guy. He had been everything he was expected to be. Son and husband, teacher and headmaster. All good. Dutiful. He was sixty-four now and he felt he deserved a rest. Only he was not getting one. Or at least that's what he was thinking as he came out of the elevator and walked to the flat across the school's roof terrace. But he would get one.

As his wife had asked him, quite a certain number of times to be honest, he had oiled the hinges of the front door earlier that day, so that she did not hear him when he came into the flat. But he heard her. She was scolding her team. Again. And again, he wondered how they could take it. And why on earth she was having these meetings in the flat. And in the evening. OK, *her* flat, and in *her* school, but this also happened to be where *he* lived. To suit *her*. *She* had decided not to retire despite what they had planned. She would probably die in that school.

'I've been a school director for twenty-eight years now,' he could hear her saying as he remained standing silently in the hall. 'And I really don't expect you to tell me how I should do my job. I have another year to go before I retire and I intend to run this school as I have for the past seven years. The year has only just started, I'm neither gone nor going yet.'

A pause.

'Hopefully I'll be staying for another two years if my dumb husband can wait even longer for me to retire,' she added.

'Jesus,' he thought, clenching his fists. He was used to taking it in. He took a step back, opened the door again and slammed it shut.

'Evening, everyone,' he said, showing just his head through the living room door for the members of the renowned Photography Institute bloody steering committee to see him.

'Hi, Michel,' they all said; all except his wife Gloria.

'Michel, do you really have to slam that door each time you come in?' she said. 'And please do oil the hinges.'

'Back in a sec,' he said. He pulled his head out of the room and stood in the hall. He tried to avoid thinking he could not take it anymore, but that was becoming more and more difficult. Pull yourself together, Michel, he told himself as he opened the spare room door and walked in. He took off his raincoat, hurled it on the double bed that occupied most of the space, and slumped next to it. 'Jesus.'

At his feet stood two large cardboard boxes he had fetched from the basement. He kicked one of them, half expecting it to complain. He bent towards the box, opened it and put the cover on the bed next to him. On top of the disordered and discouraging heap of photographs was a framed one, face down, that Michel instantly recognised. Its greyish stiff paper back bore a label that read *Daniel Beauvois, 1998*. He took the photograph out and was about to indulge in a wave of gruesome memories when Gloria barged in.

'What on earth are you doing?' she said.

'Just taking off my coat.'

'Well, put it back on, I need you to fetch pizzas from Momo and Carla's. What are these boxes now?'

'They're our old photographs. I thought I'd sort them out, you know, maybe make albums.'

'Nonsense. You do have too much time on your hands. Scan them at least so we can get rid of the boxes. And don't make a mess of the spare room.'

'Actually, I was thinking of turning it into a study to...'

'We'll see to that but now's really not the time. Pizzas...?' she said, turning around and heading back to the living room.

Michel sighed, put the photograph he was still holding on the bed and walked to the living room taking deep breaths. A few steps and there he was, smiling his impeccable smile to Gloria Beaumont-Lefort's venerable steering committee members.

'Who's in for pizzas?' he called out.

'Ha, ha, Michel, are you being our maître d' again?' Sophie Dubois, vice-director, said, in the hypocritical high-pitched voice she used when pretending to be courteous and not the bitch she was.

'I am,' he said.

'I'll have a Regina, then,' she said, and went back to her spreadsheets.

'Who's paying for this?' Nadine Laussel asked. You would think the school was run on her own money. Michel had met a lot of school accountants with that tendency but she sure was surpassing them all.

'I am, of course,' he said, smiling. Fat tight-arsed cow.

'Oh, good. I'll have a chef special with added pepperoni and fresh tomatoes.'

'I'll go with you, Michel,' Claire said.

'You will not,' Gloria snapped at her, 'we need you here.'

'Thanks, Claire,' Michel said, 'I'll manage. Goat's cheese and oregano, as usual?' he added, trying to compensate for his wife's meanness to her loyal technical director and friend for fifteen years.

'Yes,' she smiled.

'I'll have a Napolitana,' Richard broke in. 'And I'm coming with you. I have to get a file I left in my car, anyway.'

Michel noticed no one had anything to say to this. Richard, senior lecturer in the history of photography and the school's head of curriculum, would not have anyone tell him what he could or could not do.

Michel half-smiled. Fuck you, ladies.

'Let's go, Michel,' Richard said.

'What are you having, darling?' Michel said to Gloria, still trying.

'I'm not having anything. You know I don't need food.'

'I do,' he said.

—

'Thanks for giving me the opportunity to take a break,' Richard said as Michel was taking his wallet out of his raincoat in the spare room. 'That's a very nice photo,' he added, pointing to the framed photograph Michel had left on the bed.

'It is, isn't it?' Michel said, taking it and contemplating once more what he'd lost. It showed Daniel in his last school's hall, wearing his usual grey three-piece suit and colour tie. The photograph was black and white and Michel wondered what colour Daniel's tie had been that day. As ever, he was moved by the man's elegance and knew it was not just the suit. It was something he himself had never been given. He missed Daniel. But he had had no choice.

'That's Daniel Beauvois. About a year before he died. I worked as his assistant when I trained to be a headmaster in 1986. An unusually gifted man.'

'1986? You weren't always a headmaster then?'

'Oh no, I used to be an English teacher. I got tired of it. Feared I might become an old bitter teacher.' Michel put the photograph back on the bed. 'That's when I met Daniel. We'd better be going,' he said, pointing to his wife in the living room.

He held the front door for Richard and sneered at its not squeaking. He was glad Richard remained silent as they made their way across the school's roof terrace, where the staff flats stood like a series of aligned Lego blocks. But as they reached the elevator, he realised he could not face being locked in such a tiny space.

'Do you mind using the stairs?' he asked Richard.

'No problem,' Richard said.

They went down the stairs slowly, side by side.

'Daniel and I used to walk around the school at night. Well not *this* school, of course. Nothing that trendy. Just a standard middle school. Daniel would go on his round every evening after dinner, switching off that light, shutting that window. And I would follow him.'

'Still in touch?' Richard asked.

'No, he died. I told you. Killed himself,' Michel said.

'Oh my, sorry.'

'*I* found him,' Michel said. 'He had a moron of a new assistant then. That prick had taken to go on the evening rounds with Daniel. So *I'd* not been able to see Daniel in several weeks. And Daniel seemed OK with that. But I went that night. I knew the moron was finally away on a training course.'

Michel could still feel the anger as he prepared to tell the story that now sounded true, even to himself. 'As soon as I entered the school, I could feel something was not right. I simply knew something irreparable had happened and a sense of panic and deprivation took hold of me. I hurried to Daniel's office, running in the empty corridors. I thought I should run faster. But faster would have been too slow. It was too late. Everything was already lost. Daniel had been dead a while. He had shot himself.'

'Fuck. Must have been quite a shock. Why did he do that?'

'I don't know. He didn't leave a note – not one anyone has ever found. Eventually I had to stop thinking about his death for fear of going crazy.'

They had reached the street by then and were about to push the glass door to Momo and Carla's.

'Shit happens, I'm afraid. Better focus on the lighter side of life,' Richard said.

'Believe me, that's what I do.'

The door of the restaurant opened and Momo's jovial face appeared, one that always warmed Michel's heart.

'Michel, Richard, come in. What are you doing standing at the door?'

'Hi, Momo,' they both said, Richard apparently caught by the man's permanent good mood as well.

'Carla, glasses and wine.' The soothing moto.

'*Y lomo*,' Carla said as she came out of their living room, a small room with a sofa and a TV set at the back of the restaurant. She was carrying a long Spanish sausage. 'This has just arrived from my home village. You've never had anything like it.'

'Momo, better get this out of the way; we need a Napolitana – make it two, I'll have one as well, a goat's cheese and oregano, a Regina and a chef special with added pepperoni and fresh tomatoes,' Michel said.

'I bet that last one is for Nadine,' Momo said and they all laughed as Carla filled their glasses with Rioja. Life had its good moments.

—

Later that evening, as Michel was sitting once again on the spare room bed, bending over the opened box of photographs, he let out a laugh, remembering Momo's impertinent joke. Still smiling, he took one of the numerous envelopes out of the opened box. *1998–1999* it said. His smile turned wistful as he took the first photograph out.

Gloria, much much younger, hiding her nakedness under the whiteness of a cotton sheet, enamoured after they made love for the first time in that hotel in Marrakech. *Education for All: Disability, Diversity and Inclusion, an international seminar*, it had been. Gloria, smiling. Holding out her hand. Pleading eyes. Gloria begging him to make love to her, again.

He was taking another photograph out of the envelope just as Gloria appeared.

'I'll take the pizza boxes down to the bin, Michel.'

'Oh, Gloria, there's no need to do that now. It's past eleven. I'll do it tomorrow. Look,' he said. And he showed her the photograph he had made of her when they first met at the Ministry of Education's 1998 Christmas Party.

'Jesus, those were the days,' he said. 'Remember? It seems a different world altogether; no 9/11, no economic crisis, no 2002, no Charlie... Look at that party, mountains of oysters and fountains of champagne. Imagine throwing such a party on public money nowadays. It would be scandalous. And at the Great Evolution Gallery in Jardin des Plantes too. But then anything seemed possible, right-wing president and left-wing government, 'Les Bleus' world champions... Profusion and abundance, all about enjoying life. Looking back though, you could say it's a good thing the socialists enjoyed it then.'

He laughed, she didn't. She would. He carried on.

'And look at you. So beautiful in your evening dress. There I was slurping an oyster, marvelling at the line of naturalised animals, very much enjoying being part of the bright side of evolution. And there you came. Evolution made perfect. Dazzling. As majestic as the giraffe in the parade, as valuable to the human species as Buffon, Lamarck or Darwin.'

Not even a smile. Try harder.

'You turned me from ape to man.'

Still not amused. Back to an ape?

'And I couldn't resist taking the photograph with the small camera I'd brought for the occasion. And you smiled at me. And we talked through most of the night. And I promised I would call you and show you the photograph. Remember?' he said, gently taking her hand in his.

'Well, time certainly flies,' she said. 'I'll take the pizza boxes down anyway because I have to go back to my office. Don't wait up for me.' And she swiftly took her hand away from his and went.

And he was left alone, stooping, ape-like, over the photograph.

'And you loved me then,' he said. And then his eyes fell on the framed photograph of Daniel. He grabbed it and smashed it on the wall. He felt the urge to unzip his trousers and masturbate, as images of Nadine the fat tight-arsed accountant kneeling, naked, started to form in his mind and a delightful warmth loomed in the lower part of his body. He held out his hand, going for it, anticipating the pleasure of stroking his wrinkled skin, his breath cut short by the prospect of his ejaculation, the sticky expectation making his hand moist, his arse tightening as the idea of stiffness filled his mind. He could very nearly sense the to and fro movement of indulgence, hear the long moan of liberation. He could very nearly feel his face prickling and his hair standing on end as pleasure elevated his body and soul. And he could see Nadine on all four, plugged to his body, her jelly-buttocks jiggling dutifully, her fat breasts dangling submissively, her tongue spiralling dedicatedly. But he let go, he couldn't. He remained there stooping, limp.

2—*So Many Mirandas*

'Fuck,' he said out loud. Very loud.

Richard Donnary was standing by his car. Though he couldn't express it in so many words, he was waiting for something to save the evening. He'd had pizza and wine. His body had been fed but he felt unfed. He knew but would not admit the real trouble was Anna had not been there. She would not be there anymore, no one could know that better than he did. She was gone. But he would feel neither regret nor remorse. Nostalgia was good for Michel and his boxes of photographs. What was past, was past. He just told himself that had been another useless meeting. But still, it had filled his evening. It had prevented him from another long, lonely, whiskied night. But she was gone. He looked up to the director's flat on the school's roof terrace he had just left and got a vivid image of Gloria and Michel's mutual silence. Why on earth did Gloria have meetings in her own apartment? Did she have no sense of intimacy at home? He sensed his own silence creeping in and got in the car before it took hold of him.

He sat behind the wheel, fumbled with his bluetooth thingammy, got the music started and waited. He turned the key, drove very slowly to the school's car park gate, and took a right. He would have gone left had he planned to go straight home. The storm was long gone now and it was hot again. He turned left on the boulevard Arago then left again and drove very slowly until he reached the Design Bar. Outside the bar, most of his students were smoking and drinking beer out of plastic cups. Real glasses, they had been told thousands of times, were forbidden outside the bar. Another one for the environment.

'Monsieur Donnary,' they chorused as they recognised his car. 'Come and have a drink.' He parked the Jag – though parked was not the way the police would have described it; he'd have to keep an eye on it – and joined the crowd. He avoided thinking that some of them could have been his children. He had reached that age, but he would not think about it. Not now anyway. Now he was doing it again, buying booze for his students.

He entered the bar and at once remembered how he loved Paris. The smoking ban had been going on for years now but the place still smelled of cold tobacco... and French fries, and whatever it was that gave Parisian *petits bars* their peculiar smell. Pleasant mugginess, stale homeliness.

'Hey, Richard,' Thomas the bartender said. 'Same as usual?'

'Make it a double,' Richard said.

As he took the first sip of his double Laphroaig – he had a thing for Scotch single malts and she'd said, 'See, not everything's wrong about you,' and smiled that wonderful smile he'd never see again but kept seeing – he could feel someone's hand going up his back.

'It's so good to see you here,' she said.

Miranda. So many Mirandas throughout the years.

'What are you having?' he said. It seemed to him the only difference between grown-ups and well, students, was the amount of money they could spend in a bar. OK, Miranda was a postgrad student, but still.

Even the noise of them sounded young. Richard stared into his glass, his gaze getting lost in the peaty vapours of his drink, his nose relishing its amber fluidity. He felt extraordinarily static amidst the students' ebullience. Hooked onto the bar as he was, he knew his presence was a forceful one to them. It's probably the closest I'll ever get to being a father, he thought in spite of himself. Miranda swayed next to him.

'Why don't you have your camera with you, Monsieur Donnary?' she asked.

'I left it in the Jag.'

'Oh, please, go and get it and let's take a few shots.'

The students within earshot – quite a number of them, Miranda had that kind of voice – joined in. 'Oh, please, do,' they all pleaded. He gave them his amused smile and could feel in his hand the empowering rigidness of his Pentax. 'OK, I'll get it, but just a few shots and I'm off.'

As he came back, his students were already putting on their posing cloaks, except for Miranda who was putting up her Betty Boop show. Or was she just more remarkable? He let the thought go as he raised his camera to his face and took a last look at them, knowing they would instantly disappear when he'd watch them through the lens. And they did. Turning the focusing ring was like switching to an all visual world. He could not smell, he could not hear, off went their boisterous laughter, off the French fries and cold tobacco. He could just see and feel a flowing warmth as his hand went up and down the lens, focusing on their youth.

'OK, that's it,' he said, breaking the scary and delightful spell, 'I'm leaving.'

'Bye, Monsieur. Don't forget to show us the pictures when you've developed them.'

'Of course, I will, don't I always?' he said, 'and don't you forget your essay on Walter Benjamin is due next week.'

Leaving the place, he could hear them tenderly complaining.

As he walked to his car, enjoying the last echoes of warmth in his body, he heard the clatter of heels behind him and felt a pang of anxiety as he knew the story this was the first sound of.

'Would you mind dropping me off, please, Monsieur,' Miranda said, swaying more than ever.

He opened the passenger's door, put the camera back in its bag, put the bag on the back seat and held the door for Miranda to get in.

'You know where I live, don't you?' she said as he got into the car. 'It is on your way, isn't it?'

I can't believe it, he thought. And yet, he could. He'd been there before.

He drove through the familiar streets he had taken so many photos of. Street scenes of the 13ème arrondissement. Anna had laughed at his sudden urge to stop the car – in a bus lane, necessarily – and capture something he'd caught a glimpse of and just had to seize. He'd taken her home even though *she* didn't live on his way.

'Hellooo,' Miranda said, but he paid no attention. *'Hallo Spaceboy?'*

'Sorry, Miranda, it's been a long day,' he said, remembering Anna humming David Bowie.

'It's OK,' Miranda said, leaning towards the driver's seat.

He tried to stop his head from launching a Bill Withers track but on it went. *Lean on Me*. He struggled to stop it – the song, the urge – and chase images of Anna laughing at him when he started singing.

He drove faster. He had to get rid of Miranda, now. He forced his eyes to focus on the road only and soon got to her place.

She didn't move when he stopped the car, her expectancy torturing him.

He got out before she could say a word. As he went around the car, he slowly drew a line with his index finger in the dampness the rain had left on its body. At last, he opened the door for Miranda to leave.

'Off you go, young lady. Bedtime for children.' She got the message all right, smiled an 'I'll get you one day' smile, and decidedly snaked up along his body as she came out of the car. He couldn't prevent the tip of her tongue from getting to his earlobe and a long shiver from slithering down his spine, the opposite direction her body had moved. The two routes seemed to join in the same spot. He grabbed her shoulders gently and pushed her away.

'Goodnight, Miranda,' he said.

'Monsieur...' she bowed and giggled as she opened the door to her building.

Back in his car, he realised he could not go home. Not just yet. He reversed – on rue de Tolbiac, quite an unwise thing to do – and drove back to avenue d'Italie. He turned right on the rue du Docteur Laurent, rotated with the rue Damesne and entered rue Henri Pape. As he drove steadily down the road, he was happy to see the light was still on in several of the very non-Hausmanian houses. It was one in the morning, but the city never let him down. He parked his car, reached for his bag and got his camera out. He walked up and down the road, stopped under each lit window, focused and shot. He couldn't see anyone but he liked the idea that stories were unfurling behind closed doors, shut windows. He went back to the car, once more moved his hand along its slender body, sat behind the wheel with his camera in his lap and drove to the Place de l'Abbé. He parked – here again park was some sort of an approximation – and clutched the camera. As he walked around the Place, he systematically took a single shot of the halo of light under each street lamp until he came back where he'd started. He'd run out of film anyway. One, two, buckle my shoe, he thought, and drove home without stopping again.

The automatic door to his building's underground car park opened as he came close to it and he slid down the slope to his space. He remained sitting in the car for a while, feeling, as he usually did when he came out of it, that he was going out of shelter. He stroked the leather of the passenger seat, where Miranda had been sitting an hour before, where Anna had been sitting what felt like a century before. He grabbed his camera bag and left.

As he walked towards the elevator, he turned to look at the car once more. He had always dreamed of having an old Jag. There had to be some Englishness in him. 'Of course, there is, darling,' he could hear his very English mother say. She had met his father when she was twenty-one and though she had lived in France ever since she had never managed to speak French quite correctly. He spoke both languages perfectly but had always felt he was French, probably as an homage to his long dead father, developing even more chauvinism than any other Frenchman. 'Miss you, Mum,' he thought. And as he opened the front door to his apartment and turned right to put his keys on the cabinet, he came face to face with the portrait photograph he had made of his mother a few months before she died. He smiled at her. 'Thanks for everything, Mum.' And he could nearly see the portrait wink at him. That was just like her. After her death, he was informed that she had left him with the flat and the car of his dreams. He put his camera bag down, walked to the portrait and gently stroked his mother's cheek with the back of his index finger. He opened the enamel box that was on the cabinet underneath the portrait and took the letter out. He unfolded it and read it, yet again.

My beloved son,

As I know you quite well – yes, I do, don't contradict your mother – I know it will take years for you to be able to use the money you get from my death for your own pleasure and happiness. So I am afraid I have spent part of that money. When you finish reading this letter, Maître Bonnard will give you two sets of keys. One is for your flat, rue des Frigos, in that new building you like so much. The other is for the Jag you will now be driving. I drove it myself to its space in the underground car park of your apartment building, where it is now waiting for you. I must admit even I was thrilled to drive it. It is a fantastic car. Buying these things for you has made the last months of my life a very funny adventure and I am quite confident you will like them. You will think of course I am patronising you again but you will come around it. Don't you always?

I hate leaving you alone but I like to think I'll remain with you every step of the way. You have made me a very proud and happy mother. Be happy my Richard and remember, life is about here and now.

With all my love,

Mum

Richard smiled at the memory of his mother. He looked around and once again observed she had bought the perfect apartment. He made his way to the open kitchen and filled a large glass of water at the tap. He drank it up and grimaced, grabbed the bottle of Laphroaig that was standing on the worktop and filled his glass. He walked with it to the sliding bay window and stepped on the terrace. The Seine was really peaceful. He sipped his whisky and remained watching Paris until he had emptied his glass. He went back in and upstairs to his bedroom, leaving the bay window opened. He undressed and let out a sigh of relief as he got into his bed. He set his alarm clock to 7.30. He'd had no choice but to promise Michel he would meet him at nine to give him a hand. Out of pity, he guessed. He switched off the light and fell asleep quite instantly, avoiding thinking about the day that was over.

Merle Nygate is a script editor and scriptwriter. She's worked on BAFTA-winning TV in multiple genres. Most recently she co-wrote and edited audio adaptations that won both BBC Drama and New York Festival Awards. *A Righteous Spy* is Merle's first espionage novel.

merle.nygate@btinternet.com

A Righteous Spy

Soon.

I know it will be soon because when we finished prayers this morning Abu Muhunnad's eyes were shiny; and I don't think it was irritation from the hot wind that blows sand from the south.

It wasn't anything he said, but he wasn't listening when I told him about my fast, at least not as intently as he usually does. I was describing the verse I've been reading and instead of commenting, he just nodded. That's when I saw his eyes glitter with compassion.

I'm OK. Really I am.

I wanted to say that to Abu Muhunnad this morning. I wanted him to know and be certain that I am filled with joy and grateful for the opportunity, *insha'allah*. It's as if everything I've done in my twenty-seven years has led me to this point, this place, this precise moment in time where, finally, I am going to make a difference.

CHAPTER 1

Seventy kilometres away – as the drone flies – Eli Amiram made his way to the bus stop for his morning commute. Even though he'd strolled only a short distance, from apartment to bus stop, by the time Eli arrived at the shelter he was sweating. His shirt grazed his damp neck and he could smell shower soap, deodorant and his own perspiration. The middle of May and at 7 a.m. the temperature was already hitting 28 degrees. But the heat in isolation was nothing. Humidity was the killer; the wet, dense air that trapped him in its steaming straitjacket. Eli leaned against the side of the metal bus shelter and narrowed his eyes. He tried to imagine grey London streets underfoot, grey clouds above and what it might feel like to inhale, if only for a second, cool air that hadn't been artificially refrigerated. It was too bad that Gal had taken the car to drive north to see her mother. Otherwise, he'd have been in the car looking out, not sweating like an animal.

Half a metre away a woman was shrieking into her cell phone. Eli closed his eyes. He stroked the top of his shaved head and felt the new growth on his damp skull. He supposed it could have been worse; at least the *Khamsim* was over. As far as Eli was concerned, a hard blue sky and 90% humidity was a distinct improvement.

After a few more seconds of being bombarded by the woman's conversation, Eli opened his eyes to assess the source of the voice. What he saw was a fleshy face with faded blonde hair brushed back into a bun. He knew the type. The pitch of the woman's voice was bad enough, but her heavily accented Hebrew set Eli's teeth on edge. It was like listening to Stockhausen's *Helicopter String Quartet*.

Now she was dictating a shopping list and Eli pictured a shadow husband perched at a fold-down table in a kitchen where no dirty plate dared rest for more than five seconds. Fifty metres away the bus came into sight. Commuters became restive, shuffled feet, adjusted bags, found fares.

'I gotta go, *motek*,' the grandmother said. 'I'll call when I get to the hospital, I'll let you know, and don't forget to phone for the results, OK? Or the chicken.'

Poor guy, Eli thought. The bus screeched to a halt and Eli peeled his back away from the bus shelter. With calculation, not courtesy, Eli let the grandmother lumber ahead of him so he wasn't sitting next to her. The plan worked. Hauling herself aboard she found a seat halfway down the aisle. Eli made his way to an empty seat at the back of the bus. It was well away from the grandmother but next to a *dati*. Sliding down, Eli glanced over at the grey sideburns, wispy beard and pallid skin.

The bus jolted away and Eli's head jerked back against the headrest. He felt a finger nudging his ribs. Turning, Eli caught a blast of a gastric disorder from the man's mouth.

'You speak English?' The old man said. 'Or Yiddish? *Redstu Yidish*? His accent was pure Ameridish, his tone peremptory and he didn't wait for an answer. 'Is this Rosh Pinna Street? Is this the corner of Rosh Pinna and Ariel?'

'Next stop,' Eli said.

'You'll tell me when we get there.'

'Of course, it will be a pleasure.' Aware that he'd used the right idiom, Eli was nonetheless irritated with himself because he always struggled with the precision and physical placement of an English accent. The focus wasn't around the lips and vestibule of the mouth like French, neither was it located near the hard palate and throat like Arabic.

Five minutes later, when Eli was still trying to select an appropriate expression to practise on the American, they were at Rosh Pinna Street. Eli stood up to let the man out.

'Take your time, sir,' Eli said. 'There's no rush, no rush at all.' Shit. He'd done it again. Rolled the 'r'. As he sat down, Eli grimaced trying to achieve the oral position for a non-rolling 'r'.

That was when he noticed a new passenger, a woman, step into the body of the bus.

Eli stared. In dark blue jeans and flowing green top, the woman was out of proportion. Skeletal shoulders sat atop a lumpy waist and an ugly hat shaded her face. But it wasn't the absence of any aesthetic that made the base of Eli's neck prick as if an elastic band had flicked against his flesh. It was her expression.

Eli glanced across the aisle at a soldier to see if his combat receptors had kicked in but the kid was more interested in the horse-faced girl by his side. No back-up there.

Up ahead, the woman was hauling a black-and-white shopping trolley down the aisle. Judging by her strained expression the load was heavy. Eli stood up to get a better look at her.

Was she ill?

Beneath heavy make-up the woman was pouring sweat. She was

drenched. A slick of moisture dewed her upper lip and the armpits of the green blouse were dark green, almost black. OK, it was hot outside and OK, she'd dragged a loaded shopping trolley to the bus stop, but there was something wrong with her. Between two thick eyebrows there was a deep frown crease and her eyes flicked around the bus, not settling, not making contact.

Eli reached into his pocket for his cell phone. He glanced down and fingered the button to call the emergency services. Was he over-reacting? Up ahead he saw the woman's lips were moving and her hand was clenched so tightly around the handle of the shopper that he could see her knuckle ridges stand to attention.

Eli looked from his cell phone in his hand to the nearest camera in the bus, wondering if anybody was watching in real time. Hoping that some sharp-eyed kid had seen the hat that hid the woman's face. Hoping that whoever was in front of the screen had logged it and already radioed the driver. Hoping... But it wasn't enough – just to hope.

She'd found a seat. Right in the middle of the bus. Right where a device would cause the maximum damage. As she sat down Eli got a good view of her back and the narrow profile of her shoulders atop the billowing green top. Her waist was out of proportion to the rest of her body and she was holding on to that damn shopper as if her future depended on it.

The woman in the hat was nervous. She had positioned herself in the middle of the bus and that green blouse was concealing something. Eli slid out from his seat and pushed his way along the aisle towards her.

'*Slicha*, excuse me,' Eli said as he shoved aside a schoolboy standing in the aisle reading a Kindle.

Ahead, the woman was still clutching the shopper and positioning it with both hands. Not one. Struggling to keep it upright. Eli was two metres away from her and closing in when a man, an office worker in a white shirt, slid out from his seat into the aisle and blocked Eli's way. In one hand he had a paper cup of coffee and he was reaching to take a linen jacket off the seat hook with the other. Using the flat of his hand against the man's chest, Eli pushed him back into his seat. The coffee went flying as the office worker lost his balance and fell on top of another man reading a newspaper.

'What the fuck!'

Eli didn't look back.

The bus grunted to a halt and the brakes squealed. The doors hissed open. Eli reached the woman and wrenched the shopper from her grip. He glimpsed the fear in her eyes. Behind him people stood, about to get off. Eli blocked them. He ripped open the Velcro cover of the shopper and dived his hand inside. He pulled out a nightdress and a toilet bag. He tossed them across the floor of the bus where they skittered under the seats.

'What's going on? What's happening, why can't we get off?' Sharp and anxious voices. Voices close to panic. Closing in. Meanwhile, Eli plunged his hand deeper into the shopper again and again but found only softness against his assault. No wire, no block, no bomb. In his peripheral vision Eli saw the soldier boy holding back the passengers.

'What's happening? Is there something wrong? Why can't we got off?' Eli heard from the crowd of commuters.

'*Bitachon*, security,' Eli said. 'Everything's under control.'

Now on his feet Eli dragged off the woman's hat. Tear tracks striated the make-up on her face. He also saw fear, anguish and... Eli saw pain.

'Are you out of your mind? What do you think you're doing?'

That voice, that awful accent, it was the browbeating grandmother sitting right next to the innocent girl Eli had just assaulted.

'I had reason to believe—' Eli said.

Her face was red and one of her dockworkers' arms was around the girl's skinny shoulders.

'Didn't the good Lord give you eyes in your stupid big head? The girl's sick, she's going to the hospital and she's frightened to death.'

'Lady, we all have to be vigilant and aware of security at all times. D'you understand? OK, I made a mistake, I apologise, but I was acting in the best interest of everybody.'

There were rumblings from the other passengers. They were divided. Eli saw the man with coffee stain across a white shirt. He got it; he understood. But the grandmother didn't.

'What kind of idiot are you?'

He hissed, 'The kind of idiot who is trying to protect you from being blown to pieces. Do you have a problem with that?'

'*Maspeek*, enough, please,' whispered the girl through tears. 'It's OK, I'm OK.' Meanwhile the grandmother's face started to go from red to purple and her eyes bulged.

'Lady, I'm sorry, I made a bad mistake,' Eli grabbed a handful of clothes from the floor and dumped them on the girl's lap. Then, since the soldier boy was still holding back the rest of the passengers, Eli scrambled down the stairs on to the street.

He walked the rest of the way to the office.

CHAPTER 2

Ten minutes after Eli had escaped the bus, he stepped through a set of automatic doors into the blessed chill of a downtown mall. It was a relief. The incident on the bus was unfortunate; unpleasant but defensible. Eli strode past the small café where the gym bunnies hung out. As usual, he pulled in his gut. Next he passed a branch of Bank Leumi and a small supermarket with a metal turnstile and cliffs of cut-price vodka. Finally, Eli reached the north-west corner of the mall and a scuffed metal door that bore no sign. As he did every office day, Eli curled his right hand around the vertical handle and contacted the fingertip recognition keypad. Hand in position he looked around the mall, checking to see if there was anyone nearby. It was unnecessary as there were cameras everywhere but it was procedure. It's what you did; it's what you were trained to do.

Periodically refurbished and updated, this particular Tel Aviv facility was located in a building within another building. It had its own generators, electronics and water supplies, communications, cryptography and the rest of the technical tricks department. While Eli visually swept the mall, his vital signs were being monitored, fed into the computer system, compared to a set of algorithms and minutely measured to see whether he was unusually stressed or unusually unresponsive.

The door clicked open and Eli slid into the first security section where he handed in his home cell phone to the staff behind the desk and had a further retinal identification check.

As always, Eli was struck by how quiet it was when the door to the mall shut behind him. It wasn't just a door – it was a boundary; like walking from the beach into the sea to take that first breath through the snorkel into another world. Here the atmosphere was sterile, the only colour was the lights from the bank of monitors against the white wall, the only sound, apart from human voice, the hush and hum of electronics. Beyond the reinforced door, the mall shrieked with its discordant colours, tinny music and neon pleas to purchase.

Eli assumed his easy, affable, professional face. The one he used in the field, when he didn't want to share his thoughts.

'Good morning, one and all,' Eli said.

'Morning Eli,' Ze'ev, a curly haired blond boy didn't look up from the machine that was scanning Eli. 'See the game last night? Disaster.'

'There's only one team in this country, Ze'ev. Maccabi Tel Aviv is and always has been a better team.'

Ze'ev glanced away from the scanner to roll his eyes while a young woman stepped out from behind the desk and ran a second-hand scanner over Eli who stood with his legs apart and arms above his head.

Pronounced clean, Eli made his way through two more double doors to the lift and the second floor canteen.

The canteen was modern with pale wood, stainless steel and deftly placed mirrors to give the illusion of light even though the space was enclosed by metres of blast proof concrete. There were a few windows in the building but those were on the upper floors where department heads had their offices, not in the 24-hour canteen where everybody ate, from the cleaners to intelligence analysts to signal collectors, to the tech geeks, to the shrinks. The single canteen was a nod to the dim collective memory of kibbutz life where the cowshed worker sat next to the nursery nurse who sat next to the kibbutz administrator.

Pushing the wooden door open, Eli caught the scent of fresh coffee. He also spotted Rafi sitting on one of the blue plastic chairs right near the coffee station.

Eli joined the queue at the pastry station for a Bulgarian cheese *boureka*, and kept his back to Rafi to avoid eye contact. It had only been four short weeks since Rafi had been let loose on the mid-Africa desk and already he'd created something of a stir in the office. Maybe it was his leather biking jacket and white T-shirts but apparently the girls in Collections had coined a name for Rafi: 'movie star' is what they called him. Eli wondered if they had a name for him too. Best not to think too hard about that.

The server gave Eli the hot pastry wrapped in greaseproof paper; the butter from the filo smudged the package. Walking towards the coffee station, Eli kept his eyes locked straight ahead as if he was lost in some meditative thought.

'Eli, my main man,' Rafi called over in mid-Atlantic English. '*A'hlan*,' he continued in street Arabic, and finally in Hebrew, 'Eli, sit for a moment, great to see you. So, tell me, what's going on with Redcap? I just read the London signal in the summary. Looks pretty serious to me.'

Using an outstretched leg, Rafi pushed out one of the blue chairs. It was an invitation to sit down; Eli remained standing and with deliberation helped himself to the coffee at the dispenser.

'Patience, Rafi,' Eli said. 'As Tolstoy said, the two most powerful warriors are patience and time.'

CHAPTER 3

By the time that Eli stepped into the meeting room he'd worked out both tactics and strategy for dealing with Redcap.

It was no big deal. Just a manifestation of the perennial problem with agents: you might even say it was 'the nature of the beast.' Pondering the provenance of the English idiom, Eli settled himself in his usual chair with his back against the wall. In keeping with the organisation's current culture, there was no magisterial boardroom table down the middle of the meeting room and no refreshments either. Just a few Ikea side tables stacked for convenience and you brought in your own coffee.

While Eli waited for Yuval to arrive, he massaged his eyebrows with thumb and middle finger. In spite of Rafi's gleeful anticipation that the Redcap fallout would spatter in his direction, Eli was sanguine. He was not about to get wound up by this new guy's attempt at dramatisation and disruption.

Eli checked his watch and on cue, 0800, Yuval marched into the room. About the same height as Eli, or perhaps a little shorter, Yuval was dark. In the field he passed himself off, with some success, as Spanish. Thick black hair flopped over his forehead and he repeatedly and impatiently pushed back the fringe with one of his small nail-bitten hands.

In the style of a platoon leader briefing his squad, Yuval picked up the remote control and activated the screens. The logo and motto of Mossad came up and the representatives of the fourteen operational desks sat up to attention. There were no preliminaries, no chit-chat, no social niceties. Yuval was direct and interrogatory. Each day at 0800 and ten seconds for the last three months, he'd circumnavigated the room in the same order, starting with aleph – for Africa.

'The situation is like this,' Yuval started. 'We have a special operation underway in Nairobi,' Yuval punched out the words with a Sephardi Hebrew accent, his eyes pecked at his audience. 'The target has now been located and identified. There's been subsequent verification by two independent witnesses. We're only waiting for the Prime Minister's authorisation before we go. Rafi, this is your desk, do you have anything to add?'

Rafi stood up and took charge of the remote control and an image of a thick-set, suntanned man with unnaturally white teeth appeared on the screen. He was crinkling his eyes against bright sun and in the background blurred blue sea picked up golden strands of light.

'This is Klondyke,' Rafi said. 'Main supplier of military spares to Al Shabab and Hamas's long-time go to man for quality detonators. Recently he's been looking to trade up and invest in laser technology.'

Then Rafi reeled off the resources that had been made available for the operation, the estimated time of completion, the training hours the squad had completed and the three fall-back plans.

Eli was impressed. He uncrossed his legs and leaned forward, elbows on knees. All the facts and figures tripped off Rafi's tongue and as he held the floor, Yuval's head bobbed in tiny movements of comprehension and approval.

Rafi went on: 'As discussed on Friday and signed off, the tactical decision is for the squad to use a location five K from the contact point.'

'Are they going to rehearse access in situ?' Yuval said.

The subtext in the simple question was clear; no mistakes would be tolerated.

Rafi said, 'No. They've done timed rehearsals at the country club but nothing in situ.'

The country club was the jargon for the facility to the north of Tel Aviv where the special operations section was based. There were hangars of equipment, fake sets that looked like streets in different cities, flight and car simulators, not to mention the gyms, swimming pools and a prime stretch of beach for the squad to lounge about on between ops.

Yuval frowned, 'Why not?'

'I thought about it, Yuval,' Rafi said. 'But if the squad rehearses in situ the risk increases exponentially. The op area has a population density of 450 per kilometre. The Nairobi police may be corrupt but they are not inept.'

Eli had another moment of chagrin. Rafi not only knew his stuff but he was ready to stand his ground.

Rafi went on, 'It will take twelve minutes maximum to get from contact point to swamp. It's a decent road, unlike some in the area. The team will be in and out in two hours.'

On cue, a satellite image of the road appeared on one of the screens. On another there was a ground view image. On the third, the route from the contact point and on the fourth screen – on the fourth some joker had projected a still of a crocodile. Jaw open; conical white teeth; teeth primed to rip apart human flesh. Eli saw Yuval's black brows twitch into a frown.

'OK.' Yuval recovered and did one of his bird-like nods. 'Klondyke disappears. No questions and no comeback – the way we like it. Good work Rafi. Next Canada, home of the Mounties.'

Yuval moved swiftly around the room getting updates throughout the world, Far East and Australia, the US and finally, Eli's desk, Western Europe.

Yuval checked the diving watch that dwarfed his hands and sped up his delivery, 'So, the situation is like this. Redcap, an asset in GCHQ for the last fifteen years, has refused to work with his third new case officer, Gidon. Eli, what's your plan?'

Eli stood up. He didn't bother to take possession of the remote control because he hadn't had time to upload any images. And after all, everybody knew what GCHQ looked like. He brushed his hand across his scalp. 'We have two choices. One, we bring Redcap over here, give him a nice dinner, say thank you very much and retire him or two – we find someone he will work with. Yes, his product is consistently good and no, we don't have anyone else in GCHQ at his level but...'

Eli paused for effect. 'Redcap has never become the agent of influence we always hoped he would be. What's more, the older he gets the less likely it is that he'll ever get a job that involves policy-making. And that's because he's unpredictable. Fifteen years ago he walked into the London embassy because he was passed over for promotion. He has no Jewish connections, no friends, no family, no nothing but he wanted to do the thing that would make being passed over more tolerable for him. But, bottom line, there is a reason why Redcap didn't get promoted then or now. It's the exact same reason he came to us and didn't go to the SVR. He's unpredictable.'

'All agents are unpredictable. That's part of their charm,' Yuval said.

'Yuval, I'm the first person to agree with you. That's exactly what I say to the kids in training. Agents are liars, losers, fuck-ups, we all know that, but there's a fine line between being unpredictable and being unmanageable.'

'No agent is unmanageable, Eli. It's just a question of finding the right handler. It's like dating, sometimes it works, sometimes it doesn't. You know that as well as anyone. In truth, better than anyone.'

'I think you're missing the point. We need to get on with the work without looking over our shoulder waiting for the next disaster,' Eli said.

Yuval brushed back the hair on his forehead and smiled, 'Let me worry about that. You concentrate on Redcap. Start thinking about how to manage him because we've got no one else in GCHQ.'

'But we can't control him,' Eli said. 'He's an accident waiting to happen.'

'Who says?'

Eli waved a sheet of paper in Yuval's direction. 'This is the expert's report after Redcap's last debrief. That's when he got drunk and smashed a glass coffee table in the safe house. The experts say he has an undiagnosed personality disorder and paranoid narcissism.'

"The experts" was the catch-all expression used for the psychologists, psychiatrists and assorted brain suckers that were an integral part of the organisation. The CIA and FBI loved their polygraphs, the Brits relied on regular vetting panels and Mossad had their shrinks; platoons, brigades, whole fucking armies of them.

'Experts,' Yuval waved the piece of paper away, not deigning to read it. 'They've got a name for everything. Redcap has a drink or two and an accident. So what?' He brushed his hair back and checked his watch, '*Yallah*, Eli, we're out of time. We're gonna park this for the minute and you and Rafi will meet in my office in one hour. After I've spoken to the Prime Minister and got the Nairobi green light.'

Papers were moved and chairs shuffled back as everybody who was seated stood up to go. But Yuval wasn't quite done. With one of his stubby fingers he stabbed at the wall screens, 'Rafi, that is unacceptable. A killing must be pure.'

On the way out of the meeting Eli found himself walking beside Rafi who seemed quite undiminished by Yuval's growl about the crocodile.

'Can I buy you a coffee?' Rafi said. 'We've got some time before we go see Yuval.'

'Sorry, I've got a few things to do,' Eli said.

Rafi put his hand on Eli's shoulder. The weight was uncomfortable.

'Eli, come on,' Rafi said. 'Just a coffee, we've got some stuff to talk about before we have the meeting.' The big man shifted from foot to foot, he was smiling. 'I've got some information you might find interesting.'

'What's that then?' Eli said.

'Come and have coffee and I'll tell you.'

'Stop behaving like a kid with a secret. If you want to tell me something then do it,' Eli said.

'OK,' Rafi took his hand away. Eli looked up at him. At that moment, Eli thought just how easy it would be to hit Rafi somewhere between his hazel eyes, or as an alternative, aim for Rafi's Adam's apple at the precise point where a sharp punch might, if Eli were accurate, kill him.

'You have ten seconds to tell me why you want to have coffee,' Eli said.

'We're going to London,' Rafi grinned. 'That's why Yuval wants to see the both of us. And it's going to be big; really big.'

'London?' Eli said. 'It's not your account, you've only ever worked there as a bag boy; you don't know anything about the place, the politics, the culture. Why on earth would they want you in London?'

'Because I have a connection there. I have a connection with the woman we need to do the op.'

CHAPTER 4

'I'm from London Finance,' Petra said. 'Here to interview Andrew Canadell.'

She stood in the all-white reception area while the man behind the desk, who looked as if he'd used pumice stone to shave, wrote out a visitor's badge and slipped it into a plastic sleeve.

'There you are, Miss, if you just take a seat, I'll tell them you're here.'

It hadn't been hard getting the interview. Not when Petra had said that London Finance was doing a series about leading CEOs. The PR department had leapt at the opportunity to give Canadell a four-page spread in the independent journal.

Five minutes later Petra was shepherded to the twentieth floor and was sitting in Canadell's office overlooking London. The room smelt of wood polish and subdued wealth. Across the desk, Canadell sat framed by a floor to ceiling window with the Shard in the background piercing the sky.

Petra glanced down at the list of questions she'd prepared for the CEO; there was nothing too extreme on the list. Nothing that might make Canadell baulk at what she was saying or end the interview. Because that's not why she was there.

'Before you took over Gomax Pharmaceuticals you worked in the drinks industry,' Petra said. 'How do you feel your expertise has transferred?'

Canadell leaned back in his chair, his face was florid and his shirt collar was too small. In another life Petra could have seen him in a Hogarth etching with a wig askew. In this life he tugged a yellow patterned tie over his white shirt as if the strip of fabric would conceal his gut. On the left lapel of his charcoal suit Petra saw an enamel badge and noted the design of both tie and badge in her notes. The tie was a gift from someone he liked but who didn't know him well; it was too bright and too cheap. The badge was more complex; Petra clicked her camera pen to support her notes.

'Good question,' Canadell said. 'There are certainly transferable skills and indeed, these are both people businesses. I value...'

Petra nodded, smiling with demure respect and memorised the room. She divided it into sections as she'd been taught and noted the artefacts and objects. Later on these would be analysed to consider what they might say about Canadell and the report she produced would be sent to his business competitors. Behind him, on a small side table there was the ubiquitous family portrait, with what looked like wife number two – or perhaps even three. There was also a portrait of a school-age child on the desk. From what Petra could see, the CEO's wife was not quintessentially Anglo-Saxon; she had dark hair and high cheekbones. Perhaps Slavic; perhaps Native American. That might prove to be interesting, but so far, in this particular interview there were slim pickings.

TREVOR WOOD

Trevor Wood left the Royal Navy in 1992 and retrained as a journalist, working on several newspapers in the North East. Following a brief spell as a spin doctor he took up writing full time and has since co-written eleven plays. He lives in Newcastle with his wife Pam and daughter Rebecca.

t.wood@blueyonder.co.uk

When a Fire Starts to Burn

1

Falkland Sound, 1982
The ship's tannoy breaks the threatening silence.

'BRACE FOR IMPACT.'

Jimmy has been expecting it, the Argey Skyhawks have been buzzing over them like deadly mosquitos all morning, but hearing the words out loud still comes as a shock. That morning, one of the lads in the mess had been banging on that 'not knowing' was the worst thing but that was a pile of shite. Knowing was worse. Knowing was much fucking worse. The tannoy crackles back into life.

'BRACE, BRACE, BRACE.'

This time Jimmy reacts. He dives behind the ladder which leads up to the upper deck and wedges himself in, his back set firm against the bulkhead, knees pulled up tight to his chest, feet jammed under its base. For the first time in his brief life he's glad he's a short-arse. Christ knows where Red is but it's every man for himself now.

The impact of the first bomb hurls the stern up in the air. Jimmy shoots forward, flinging his right arm out to stop his head crashing into the underside of the ladder. Fuck, that hurt. The second explosion is bigger. The ship lurches violently to the right and, this time, his head smashes into the steps. Inside his anti-flash hood he can feel blood pouring down his forehead into his eyes. Most of the lights have died but, through the blood, Jimmy can still see thick, black smoke pouring down the passageway towards him. It is so hot his ears are starting to sweat.

He jams his eyes closed, puts his hands over his ears, and takes a deep breath to suck in clean air before the smoke overwhelms him. A sickly-sweet smell, like burning pork, hits him. The gut-wrenching screams echoing down the passageway, where the first-aid team are stationed, tells him exactly what that means.

The ship is vibrating noisily, like a giant tuning fork. A brief image of Bev in widow's black flashes into his head. He mutters a prayer to a God he usually mocks, but before he has got to 'Hallowed be thy name' he feels a tug on his shirt. He opens his blood-sticky eyes. Red's face is inches from his, his mouth opening and closing silently. Jimmy takes his hands off his ears. His friend's high-pitched Scouse accent penetrates the hissing and crashing of the ventilation pipes collapsing around them.

'Move it lad, get up top.'

Jimmy shakes his head but Red drags him out by his shirt and pushes him round to the front of the steps.

'Go! Fucking smoke'll kill you.'

Jimmy clambers up, flinching as the heat of the handrail bursts through his thin gloves. There is a sliver of daylight above him filtering through the smoke – the hatch cover has been ripped from one of its hinges and fallen to one side. He squeezes through the narrow gap.

There should be an airlock at the top with two doors but the inner door is lying on the deck and the outer has been obliterated, nothing but smouldering jagged metal, the grey paint bubbling and blistered. He lurches through the gaping hole and emerges on the port side of the ship. It stinks of sulphur and fear. Red pushes past Jimmy and races through the smoke towards the flight deck. Jimmy stands and stares over the side of the ship. There is a headless body caught in the netting.

A muffled shout jerks him into action. He chases after Red who has grabbed a fire hose and is aiming it at the flames which are shooting out of what remains of the hangar. Water dribbles from the nozzle.

'The fire main's shot,' Red shouts, 'I'd be better off pissing on it.'

Amidst the smoke Jimmy can see metal debris scattered everywhere. A brief gust of wind momentarily clears his view and he sees something else, something bigger, lying on the flight deck. He runs towards it but trips and falls, crashing heavily onto the deck. He turns and sees a pair of overall-clad legs sticking out from a fallen section of the hangar roof; one of the flight crew. He jumps to his feet and tries to pull the poor sod out, only half succeeding. Both legs have been severed just above the knee and whatever... whoever they had been attached to is still under there somewhere. The vomit comes before he can remove his hood and half of it goes back down his throat. He rips the hood off and spits the rest out.

A feral scream comes from the back of the ruined hangar.

Red drops the dried-up hose and runs towards the scream. There is a small pop and then an ear-shattering explosion. Chopper fuel. A fireball hits Red square in the chest, shooting him backwards through the air like a blazing rag doll, crashing into the guard rail.

For a moment he hangs there, a vaguely human shape in a haze of flame, a pair of orange and black arm-like shadows windmilling for balance. And then he's gone.

2

Leazes Park, Newcastle, 20 May 2012
Jimmy didn't have a watch. He liked watches well enough but they were more use as currency. The last time he'd found one, in a bin behind a big house in Jesmond, he'd swapped it for some dog biscuits. It didn't matter cos he could always tell what time it was – or near enough as makes no difference. Like now – somewhere between 3 and 3.30 a.m. He used to be more precise, always within ten minutes one way or the other he reckoned, but since they brought in the all-night licensing laws the mixture of noise and light from the bars and clubs had messed with his head and he was sometimes out by an hour or more. It was easier here though, quieter. Leazes Park wasn't his normal patch but he liked to keep on the move. It was harder to hit a moving target.

His favourite spot used to be just behind Greggs in the main street. The warmth generated by the ovens seemed to stick around all night. When you were hungry though, the lingering smell of cheese pasties could drive you insane. On the plus side you sometimes found a few in the bins, past their sell-by date but good enough for the likes of him and Dog. Then the bastards put some spikes in the ground to stop people crashing there.

This wasn't a bad spot though. The late night revellers tended to stay clear. No one really wanted to walk home through a dark park, not even the nut jobs, so the chances of someone pissing on you in your sleep were low, unlike on the street where you were invisible by day and a wanker-magnet at night.

He'd found a spot under an old beech tree behind the tennis courts where he and Dog could rest up, where no one could see him. He could see them though. There were others here, some he knew, some not. It used to be same old, same old, but new faces on the street were common now, more so during the day when the pretend beggars appeared, but even at night the numbers were growing.

He could make out a shape on the bench near the path that ran along the top of the bank, on the far side of the court, underneath the only lamp post still working. At least they hadn't fucked with the benches. A lad from York had told him that the council there had bolted arm rests onto the middle of them to stop people sleeping.

A crack from somewhere behind him made him jump. Jimmy sat up, hugging his sleeping bag around him and putting a restraining hand on Dog who was on his feet, growling softly. He looked around. Though the moon was hidden by thick clouds, his night vision was working well, one of the bonuses of sleeping like a… whatever the opposite of a baby was. An old man? A dead man? That couldn't be right, dead men sleep great.

There was nothing to be seen. A false alarm. He patted Dog on the head and the mongrel terrier curled back down near his feet.

Jimmy watched as the figure on the bench stirred in his sleep and rolled over. It was Deano. The Cossack hat was a dead giveaway. Gadge called him 'The Twat in the Hat' but Deano didn't mind cos he reckoned it was well toasty. Jimmy watched as Deano pulled his hat over his ears and rolled back down, his face turned towards the bench, the hulking shadow of St James's Park behind him, towering over the houses that flanked the park. That's when Jimmy heard the voices. Men, at least a couple of them, laughing in the distance.

Sound travels miles in the park at night so, at first, he wasn't sure where they were but then he caught a glimpse of two men through the trees by the lake, heading down past the derelict pavilion, their bright green, high-vis jackets standing out in the darkness. Coppers, Jimmy thought, pulling himself further back, well out of sight of the path.

'I wouldn't touch her with a bargepole,' one of them said.

'You haven't got a bargepole, mate,' the other one said, laughing, 'more like a Twiglet.'

As they came closer Jimmy could see them more clearly through the mesh fence surrounding the courts. The one who was still laughing was huge, like a wardrobe on legs.

'What have we got here?' the smaller copper said, spotting Deano. They were now standing underneath the lamp and Jimmy recognised the big one; he'd got previous.

'You can't sleep here, pal,' the big copper said, nudging Deano with his baton. Deano didn't move.

'Oi!' he shouted, nudging him harder, 'get up!'

Deano rolled over slowly and looked up at the pair standing above him.

'Come on cloth ears, get moving or you'll get my boot up your arse.'

Dog growled again and the smaller copper turned and peered across, towards the noise. Jimmy edged even further back into the shadows, just in case, dragging a reluctant Dog by his collar, hoping he wouldn't start barking.

'Can't I stay here just for now?' he heard Deano say in his childlike voice.

'No you bloody can't,' the big copper said, hauling Deano off the bench and, in one movement, hurling him down the steep bank into some thorny bushes next to the court fence.

'Steady on Bob, he's just a kid,' the other one said.

'Just a kid my arse, he's as old as you.'

Deano knew better than to complain. He scrambled out of the bushes, crawled up the bank and headed back to the bench.

'Where are you going?' the big copper said.

'Get my stuff,' Deano said, pointing at a small rucksack tucked under the bench.

'No you're fucking not,' the big copper said.

'But I need—'

The kick caught Deano straight in the balls. As he fell a second kick caught him on the side of the head.

'For Christ's sake, Bob,' the smaller copper said, grabbing his friend's arm. The other man shrugged him off, pulled out Deano's rucksack and heaved it over the iron railing that edged the park. He laughed and glanced down at Deano who was quietly wiping blood away from his face.

'Now piss off, you scrounging git.' He aimed another casual kick at Deano but the lad didn't need telling twice, leaping to his feet and legging it off towards the gate at the top of the path.

'Have a nice day!' the mean bastard shouted.

Jimmy watched carefully as the two policemen headed off, to make sure they left the park. Though he'd learnt the hard way that sticking your head above the parapet gets it shot off, the guilt of inaction still burnt in his throat; even Dog had moved away from him.

'Bollocks to you, Dog,' Jimmy said, 'not my fight.'

3

The Pit Stop, Newcastle, 4 June 2012

The scratches were still there. It had been a couple of weeks but Jimmy could see them on the back of Deano's hands. He'd never mentioned the kicking he got and Jimmy wondered if Deano knew he had been there, watching, doing nothing.

Gadge was telling one of his stories, something about a Salvation Army woman wanting to save him. Jimmy was only half listening, finishing his soup, which didn't taste of anything in particular but was at least hot.

'So she gave us a Bible and said "this will save you,"' Gadge said. 'I looked at her and said "that's exactly what I need." You should have seen her face. It was what's-a-name... beatific.'

Deano nodded as if he knew what Gadge was on about. Over Deano's shoulder Jimmy could see the small TV in the corner. On it there was a huge crowd of people waving tiny Union Jack flags, all standing in The Mall; Jimmy recognised it from back in the day, when he'd had to attend a Remembrance Day service in Whitehall. Doing his duty. There was a huge stage, smack bang in front of Buck House. On the stage there was a fat man in a beefeater costume stamping his foot.

Gadge was on a roll now; there was no stopping him once he got going.

'I took it off her, the Bible that is, and opened it up, pretending to read it like. She's still smiling, as if the Lord himself had stuck his tongue up her fanny. I looked up at her with gratitude and said "thank you, missus."'

'What did you do then?' Deano asked. He was probably stoned when Gadge told this story before. It was a Catholic priest last time.

'What do you think I did, Deano? I ripped out a bunch of pages and threw them on the fire. "That'll keep it going for the whole night" I said, holding up what was left of the good book. The Sally Army lass was squealing like a pig, trying to grab the rest off us. You should've heard the language. Made us blush.'

Deano thought it was the funniest story he'd ever heard. Like he did last time. On the TV Jimmy could see the Queen on stage, holding what looked like a giant diamond. She placed it in a stand and a huge flame shot up into the air. Within seconds fireworks had filled the night sky behind Buck House.

'Am I boring ya?' Gadge asked. Jimmy shook his head.

'You're boring me, ya gobshite.' A new voice. From his right. Jimmy looked at the newcomer. Long, straggly blond hair and black teeth. A smell of cheap lager and sausages. He was wearing a grey army greatcoat that looked like it had been through a war or two.

'Is that right, Goldilocks?' Gadge said to the newcomer. Gadge was practically square, short and wide, but muscular not fat. He could look after himself. All around them people were starting to move away. A stainless steel salt cellar was knocked off the table and rolled along the floor. One of the younger volunteers hovered, unsure whether to get involved.

Someone had turned the sound up on the TV, there was a loud bang as a huge firework exploded. Jimmy flinched.

'Pussy,' the stranger said.

'Him or me?' said Gadge.

'Both.'

'He doesn't mean nothing, Gadge. You d-didn't mean nothing mister, d-did you?' Deano said, his voice trembling with worry, his big urchin-like eyes opening wide – a look that earned him more money than most on the streets.

'What if I did?' the stranger said, and placed his hands flat on the table as if preparing to leap across at Gadge. Another firework exploded.

'You didn't,' Jimmy said, taking a tight grip on the man's left arm. The stranger turned to look at him. Jimmy was holding a fork, about eight inches above the man's outstretched fingers. The man tried to pull his arm away but Jimmy was too strong. He stared at Jimmy for a moment but then looked down.

Jimmy let go of Goldilocks's arm. He thought about saying something conciliatory, to give the man a chance to save face, but he'd already done more than he should have, broken his vow not to get involved, so he kept schtum. Defeated, Goldilocks slowly pushed his chair back, got up and moved away. The young volunteer breathed a sigh of relief and went back to wiping a table.

Gadge laughed. 'Fuck off with you Goldilocks before my man Jimmy kicks off for real. You wouldn't like him when he's angry.' Somehow Gadge always knew stuff, Jimmy didn't have a clue how he knew stuff but he knew stuff all right.

Jimmy reached over and grabbed Goldilocks's left-behind plate. He made sure no one was looking and put it under the table where Dog leapt on it greedily.

Back on the TV the Queen was giving it her best Mona Lisa smile while, immediately behind her, a thin, glamorous woman with dark brown hair grinned inanely.

'He's filth I reckon,' Gadge said, nodding at Goldilocks, who was now sitting on his own in the corner of the room.

'A copper?' Deano said.

'Aye, undercover.'

Jimmy thought about the man's teeth. Gadge saw conspiracies everywhere, you name it: the Moon Landings, Princess Di, 9/11, none of them what they seemed.

On the TV the fireworks had reached a crescendo, lights exploding all over the London sky. Someone had turned the volume up really loud and the room was filled with the sounds of *Land of Hope and Glory*.

Jimmy hadn't seen a sign of either for a long time.

4

Presto Supermarket, Newcastle, 1984
No matter how hard Jimmy tries, the stacks of tinned vegetables just keep on diminishing. He's been in and out of the warehouse countless times but the customers outnumber him 100-1 so he's fighting a losing battle. There are only a couple of dented baked bean tins left on the shelves and no own-brand tinned tomatoes at all, even the expensive brands are disappearing fast. Fucking Christmas shoppers.

Mr Owen, his supervisor, has already passed by twice, muttering, and it's not even lunchtime yet; it's only a matter of time before he says something, even though it's the same all over the store. Owen never hassles the full-time staff but the temps, like Jimmy, are fair game. And it's not just Owen; the customers are getting on his back too.

'Excuse me?'

Jimmy stops unloading his pallet and turns around to stare at the latest space invader.

'Where have you hidden the bread sauce?' She's definitely posh; locals make their own.

'The bread sauce?' she repeats, a little louder, like he's deaf.

'Don't know,' Jimmy finally replies and turns back to his work.

'Is that the best you can do?' she says but he ignores her. Jimmy can feel her standing behind him, waiting for him to turn around again, which isn't going to happen.

Ten seconds passes. She sighs loudly. He takes out his Stanley knife.

'Arsehole!' she exclaims. Jimmy hears her turn her shopping trolley round as she heads off in the opposite direction. He slices clean through the middle of another box, imagining it's the woman's expensive cashmere coat, and places two trays of tinned marrowfat peas on a stack. Immediately, a man grabs four of the tins and drops them in his trolley. Jimmy turns, knife still in hand and glares at him. The man scurries off down the aisle, a dodgy trolley wheel providing a discordant backing track to his escape.

An hour later it's total carnage, the shoppers fighting like sailors at last orders – a mad trolley dash with added casualties. Two blokes are facing off in the aisle, both unwilling to let the other pass; another two are fighting over the last tin of soup like relay runners wrestling with a baton change.

'It's like a war zone,' a young student-type says to his girlfriend.

'No, it fucking isn't,' Jimmy mutters, and the pair back off, the girlfriend glancing back at the Stanley knife in his hand. Someone taps Jimmy on the shoulder and he spins round, the knife still in his right hand. Owen jumps back in alarm, his eyes fixed firmly on the blade. Jimmy can't believe he let the prick sneak up on him; he has to be more careful than that, it could have been anyone.

'What's going on?' Owen says.

'Nothing.'

'I can see that,' Owen says, looking at the empty stacks. 'What the hell have you been doing all day?'

'It's busy.'

'No shit, Sherlock,' Owen says, smiling as if he's just coined the phrase. 'It's Christmas Eve, what did you expect? I told everyone at the morning briefing they'd have to up their game. Weren't you listening? It's like our Cup Final, Christmas Eve, I told you that. Twice. You need to pay attention, comprende?'

'I'm doing my best,' Jimmy says.

'Well it's not good enough. Do better or I'll really light a fire under your arse,' Owen replies.

Jimmy blinks twice.

'D'you hear me? Get on with it.'

Jimmy's forehead hits Owen smack on the bridge of his nose. Owen goes down like a puppet with its strings cut, blood gushing down over his mouth and chin. A woman with a baby in a sling screams and most of the other shoppers flee from the aisle as quickly as their overloaded trolleys will allow them. Jimmy stands above the stricken supervisor, the knife still in his hand. Owen looks up, his senses slowly recovering, fear in his eyes. He tries to edge backwards but his back is pressed firmly against the stacks of tinned veg.

'Keep away from me,' Owen says, his eyes flicking from Jimmy's face to the knife and back again.

Jimmy picks up a large carton of tomato juice from a stack on the other side of the aisle, slashes a hole in it and empties the contents over Owen's head.

'I quit,' Jimmy says, dropping the knife and the empty carton on the floor and walking past Owen, who is trying to wipe bright red juice from his eyes. A nervous-looking security guard appears at the end of the aisle and makes a lacklustre attempt to grab Jimmy's arm but he brushes past him.

'You can't quit,' Owen shouts after him, 'you're fired.'

Too late, Jimmy thinks. It was my call.

—

Jimmy sees the package on the floor as soon as he enters the flat. He puts his six-pack of Carling Black Label down and picks it up. There are several different addresses scrawled on it and crossed out. He rips it open and something shiny falls on to the threadbare carpet. A medal. The MOD had invited him to a presentation ceremony down in London months ago but he hadn't bothered to reply, didn't want the fuss. Or the memories.

He examines the medal closely. It's fake silver with the Queen's head on one side, surrounded by something in Latin. He turns it over. The Falkland Islands' coat of arms is on the reverse. He thinks about biting it – he's seen athletes do it at the Olympics – but he's no idea why, so doesn't. He's about to put it on the side table when he sees the blue, green and white striped ribbon hanging out of the torn packet. Jimmy attaches the ribbon to the medal, pins it on the overall that he's walked all the way home in, sits down in his chair, turns on the TV and opens his first can of the day.

On the TV, a man from the Open University with lank, greasy brown hair is explaining that a hole has appeared in the ozone layer. Jimmy understands about one word in three so his gaze occasionally slips to the dusty photo of his wedding which sits on top of the TV cabinet; Jimmy in his No. 1 uniform, Bev glowing in a vintage red velvet number, wearing a smile that he hasn't seen for a while. Last time was when they bought the flat – used the lump sum he got with his medical discharge – psychologically unfit for duty they said, even though there's nothing wrong with him.

—

A Christmas edition of *Grange Hill* is on now and Jimmy is laughing at the French teacher's obvious wig, five empty cans scattered at his feet. When Bev walks into the front room he jumps to his feet and salutes, spilling warm lager on the carpet

'Front room ready for inspection,' he says, even though it clearly isn't.

'I thought you were doing a double shift?' she says.

'I was,' Jimmy says, 'I quit.'

'Not again Jimmy, you promised me.'

Jimmy takes a swig from his can and then offers it to Bev.

'What do you think you're doing?' she says.

'Celebrating,' he says. 'I'm a hero.' He points to the medal, still hanging from the lapel of his overall.

'For services to Queen and Country,' he says.

'Congratulations,' she says, slumping on to the sofa. 'I've had some news as well.'

He stares at her, curious, still holding the can out.

'I'm pregnant,' she says.

The Quayside, Newcastle, 5 June 2012

Jimmy woke up with tears running down his cheeks. He didn't know why. Dog was sitting up, staring at him, confused. Jimmy had probably been shouting in his sleep. Bev used to banish him to the spare room when it got too much.

He could see the names of various cities etched into the side of the open roof: Hull, Antwerp, London, Malmo, Copenhagen. Places the ships used to go, when there were ships, when there were shipyards, right there, on the river, where his dad worked before he got laid off. Now there were only bars and expensive works of art, like this place, the Swirle Pavilion, a future folly, with its sandstone pillars, a golden globe hovering above its open top like a satellite or something.

Someone was talking, arguing even. He sat up and looked through a gap between two stone pillars. Two men stood about thirty yards away, by a two-bar rail that ran along the river, just down from the dormant cruise boats. This was tourist territory so there were plenty of working street lights and Jimmy could see the men clearly, framed in the towering arc of the Millennium Bridge.

The man facing Jimmy was tall, over six feet, donkey jacket, big boots, a black-and-white-striped beanie hat on his head, light glinting from his glasses. He reminded Jimmy of a bricklayer friend he used to have, his shoulders somehow too big for the rest of him.

The other man, facing away, was shorter and slighter, wearing a denim jacket and light-coloured chinos, longish dark hair, a black bag – like a school satchel – slung over his shoulder. A social worker type, Jimmy thought, and he'd met enough of them to know.

There was no one else around. The nearby bars and restaurants had long since kicked out their punters. About 4 a.m. Jimmy reckoned.

The men were closer together now, talking, the smaller one shrugging occasionally, slightly unsteady on his feet. Jimmy wondered if it was a gay hook-up but if it was they were in the wrong place. Everyone knew Dogleap Stairs was the place for that. Anyway, none of his business.

He lay down again, drifted off.

Flames everywhere. He's in bed. An empty space beside him. Burning curtains fall to the floor, setting fire to the bed covers. He leaps up, naked, sweating.

Where's Bev? The doorway and window are ablaze. A woman's scream from somewhere. The stairs? He runs through the doorway, feeling no heat, no pain, straight into the back of Bev who is standing on the landing. But it's not the landing. It's the flight deck, the South Atlantic all around them. He spins her around. Her hair is on fire, lips and nose melting.

'Get help,' she whispers, locking him in a fiery embrace.

Jimmy woke again, bathed in sweat, his heart pounding, ready to burst out of his chest like in *Alien*, his hands beating at the non-existent flames, his eyes searching for Bev but seeing only open sky. Dog stirred at his feet, disturbed by both Jimmy's movement and the raised voices outside, angrier than before.

'You're wrong,' one of the men shouted.

'Don't think so.'

Jimmy took a deep breath and let it go, then another and another, until he felt his heartbeat slow. A cellmate had once told him that thinking of a happy place would help. 'Like where?' he'd asked.

Suddenly there was another shout, indistinct this time, then a cry of pain and a thud, something heavy hitting the ground. Jimmy froze. Someone else's problem. Under his breath, he repeated his self-taught mantra.

'Not my fight. Not my fight. Not. My. Fight.'

The sudden silence bothered him more than the shouting and he wished the voices would start up again. Then he heard another noise, a dragging sound, something heavy being pulled along the ground and wished it was silent again.

'Not my fight,' he whispered.

To his relief the dragging sound stopped. The loud splash that followed was worse though. Jimmy took one more deep breath, sat up slowly and looked across to where he'd last seen the men. The bricklayer was on his own now, his back to Jimmy, standing at the rail and peering at the river. The other man – the social worker – had vanished, his satchel left lying on the ground. After a few minutes, the tall man turned, picked up the bag and left.

As soon as he was out of sight Jimmy went to the rail, Dog at his heels, and looked over. There was nothing to see; just the black waters of the River Tyne, still as a grave.

CAROLINE JENNETT

Caroline Jennett lives in Potters Bar and works as a property managing agent. Her current novel *Where Did You Sleep Last Night?* is set across two timelines and draws upon her experiences as a twenty-first century mother and a chalet maid in Jersey, Channel Islands in the 1990s.

carolinejennett@aol.com

Where Did You Sleep Last Night?

I am not a murderer.

CHAPTER ONE

It's late Saturday night and there's a knock at the door; three raps, a pause and the same again. She's forgotten her keys.

Graham stirs, 'Sounds like a proper copper's knock, that. Do you mind, love?' He settles back to watch the penalties.

I go to open the door, expecting Holly. But it is the police.

'Is this the residence of Holly Roberts? May we come in?' they ask.

I stand aside from the door and they come in. They insist I sit so I drop down next to Graham on the sofa. I see my own fears for the worst reflected in his face. Neither of us speak. We can't

'Holly's been sexually assaulted. She's at the hospital now,' the police say. 'Bring her some clothes.'

Not dead then, thankfully not dead. I pack a bag for life and we leave within ten minutes of their arrival.

Out in the street a pale blue Fiat screeches to a halt. The back door opens and a girl tumbles out and lurches into the gutter looking for something. She is beneath the streetlight and I can see she has long dark hair and is wearing a tight black dress with a slit up her thigh. For a moment I think it's Holly. She leans down and retrieves a shoe and holds it above her head triumphant. No, she's taller than Holly, not so slim. The driver revs the engine and keeps pulling away. Graham tugs me gently by the elbow and I climb into the back of the police car.

The police stop right there on the yellow hatches and we follow them into Accident and Emergency. My feet are cold from forgotten socks as we pass through nameless corridors of brown-tiled floors and cream-tiled walls. Posters punctuate the wall space advertising drug awareness facilities and SEPSIS. We pass through the canteen at the centre of the ground floor. A little girl with black hair and red ribbons raises her ted's paw and waves it at me as we scurry past. The adults around the table with her lean into each other, heads almost touching, whispering urgently to each other, dabbing noses as their tea stagnates. We reach the end of the corridor and turn right.

A bluish hue from fluorescent strip lighting makes everything look sick, even the furniture. A door to our left bursts open and a young doctor rushes past us, his stethoscope flying out behind him. He signals an apology as he races around the next corner.

Before I can gather myself, the police stop at a set of double doors with white-out porthole windows. I catch the glimpse of a woman's reflection, a dark halo of frizz around a pale face. It takes a moment to recognise myself.

'In here,' the police say.

I see Holly as soon as they open the door. She is behind a screen but I can see she is conscious; she is sitting up and a nurse is with her. She has a beige blanket wrapped around her shoulders. I'm not sure if she is shivering or crying. At the sound of the door opening the nurse stands up and pulls the curtain to behind her.

'And you are?' she asks.

'Mr and Mrs Roberts,' and 'Gemma, Holly's mum,' Graham and I say at the same time. The nurse stands aside and I rush to my daughter and hold her tight. Make-up streaks down her face. There's no blood, none that I can see. She's trembling and so pale; I hold her until she is still. I relax my grip but she clings to me, not yet ready to be released. The nurse stands silently twisting a diamond ring on her left hand with the index finger and thumb of her right. Graham hangs back, wringing his hands, eyes darting from floor to ceiling, not knowing where to look.

The nurse introduces herself to us. Her name is Clare. She is chubby and jolly and she tells us she has bagged up Holly's clothes so we needn't worry about that. Holly wears a hospital gown tied at the back of her neck. She's still cold she says, so Clare goes to fetch an extra blanket and leaves us on our own.

'What's happened?' I ask, my voice a squeak.

'I'm sorry,' Holly whispers.

'Shush, you don't need to be sorry.' I reassure her. 'What happened, love?'

She tries to speak again but Graham places his hand on her shoulder. 'Leave her be,' he mouths at me.

'We'll get through this, love,' he says. I shake my head, and clamp my lips together. I can't speak; my throat too dry, my voice unsteady.

Nurse Clare returns with the blanket. Graham and I instinctively withdraw.

'There you go, duck.' Clare tucks Holly's legs in under the blanket. 'Have you told Mum and Dad what's going on?'

Holly shakes her head, a curtain of straight black hair covers her face.

'Shall I, then?' Nurse Clare faces us and explains, 'Holly has been attacked. We need to do some tests on her and carry out the Rape

Evaluation Procedure.' At the word 'rape' Graham crushes my hand but I can barely feel him. I look at Holly but she's keeping her head down. I can't see any bruises and she doesn't seem to be in any pain. Holly's face is obscured by a curtain of hair. I want to scoop her up and comfort her. I want to run her a bath and make her beans on toast. I want to tell her it will be all right, that I know what she's going through.

Clare continues. 'We try to keep the procedure as un-intrusive as possible, but due to the nature of the allegation the examination will be very intimate.' I try to catch Holly's eye, but she won't meet my gaze. I want her to know that it is not her fault. She's done nothing to be ashamed of.

'Sit up straight for me now,' Clare says. She confirms Holly's name and date of birth and snaps on blue disposable gloves. Clare sections off her hair with black plastic clips like she's doing foils and takes a nit comb through it, section by section. Every time Clare hits a snag, she wipes the comb's teeth clean and bags the tissue. She tries to be gentle but I see Holly wince more than once.

'There you go, duck. That's the most painful part over with already. Wasn't so bad, was it?' Clare goes to rub Holly's head in a gesture of affection but Holly recoils before the touch reaches her. 'It's all right, Holly, you just lie down for a minute and try to relax.' Clare takes a sticker from the clipboard at the end of Holly's bed, slaps it on the bag of tissues and seals it. 'I just need to comb through down below, then you'll be ready for Doctor. Mr Roberts, I am going to have to ask you to wait outside.'

Graham is halfway out of the door before she's finished her sentence. I'm surprised he lasted as long as he did.

'You'll stay with me?' Holly asks. I squeeze her hand; her fingers are icy. I nod, of course.

'Just part your legs for me, duck,' Clare says. 'That's it, keep your knees down for a minute.' She pulls Holly's gown up and places the blanket on her belly. I can see Clare's face but not her hands. I feel Holly grip my fingers.

'You all right, Mum?' she asks, concerned. I realise I am crying. I wipe my cheek and black spots of mascara smear the back of my hand.

'Look at us,' I say. 'A right pair of doughnuts.' Holly smiles and then gasps in pain.

'Sorry, love. Bit tender is it?' Clare looks up at us as she bags another tissue. 'Nearly done, just raise your knees for me.' She drops another tissue parcel of pubic hair stuck together in a clump into the bag of evidence.

She's just finishing up, placing her little bags into the yellow sack tied off on the trolley when the doctor arrives. The doctor wears high-heeled patent leather boots under the white coat of her authority and tells us her name is Marcia. She sits opposite us on the chair at the foot of Holly's bed. 'I need to examine Holly and take some samples. Also, I need to carry out a colposcopy, for which I need your consent.' She speaks to me, not Holly. I think, from her accent, she is Portuguese.

I clear my throat. 'What is it?' I ask.

'We insert a camera to examine the uterus and surrounding area. The procedure is quite painless, but there may be some discomfort. Some patients report a slight pinching, no worse than a smear test.' Holly has no frame of reference. She looks to me for reassurance. Marcia misreads the look. 'It's crucial for gathering evidence.'

'No big deal, Hols,' I say. Not very nice though, I think. I sign the form.

Dr Marcia scrubs up and snaps on blue disposable gloves. She selects a six-inch-long stick, like a cotton bud tipped with a white rubber comb which she inserts into the crevice between Holly's teeth and cheek. She uses five sticks in total and with each one she narrates a fresh description of an oral location. Beside her, Clare notes every comment and bags the evidence of Holly's mouth. More than once Holly gags and when Marcia takes a sample from the back of Holly's tongue, I fear she will throw up over the doctor's hand.

She stops gagging when they finish and Nurse Clare says, 'Just need to pop your feet in here.' She straps Holly into the stirrups. I sit with Holly holding her hand as she lies flat on her back with her legs spread open. Marcia is at the end of the bed with another handful of swabs.

'I'm just going to swab you again. You may experience some discomfort, I'll be as gentle as I can.' Holly nods and looks at me questioningly. Marcia begins, 'Some tearing to the right side labia majora and bruising to minora.' Clare notes her comments and Holly winces as Marcia takes swabs. I count ten swabs then catch sight of Marcia bagging a blood stained sample and have to look away. Marcia murmurs 'Not long now,' from the space between Holly's legs.

Clare seals the bag shut and I think they will let Holly put her legs down but they don't. Instead Marcia squirts gel into her gloved hand and wipes it onto Holly's vagina.

'It's cold,' Marcia says.

'I know,' Holly replies.

Clare drags a trolley out from the corner of the room and sets it up at the foot of the bed. Marcia positions the legs of the miniature telescope so it is at exactly at the right height for Holly and zooms in. On the monitor beside Holly's bed a circle of livid red on pulsing pinkness appears.

'OK, a small tear on the right labia minora. Hymen ruptured but not recently. No obvious signs of bruising to the vaginal walls. Small rupture to the cervix.' Clare notes the comments. I try to understand what they are saying but the words 'rupture' and 'tear' keep ringing round my head.

'Does it hurt, love?' I ask.

'Not really, you know,' she shrugs. No, I don't know. I've never had the procedure.

They let her out of the stirrups when the colposcopy is finished and make her kneel on all fours. Her gown is open at the back and it hangs down, the lower half of her body exposed.

'This may cause you some discomfort, Holly. We need to take some swabs from your anal region.' Holly doesn't seem to care anymore. She is still as they insert the first swab. She takes deep breaths in and deeper ones out to stay calm. Holly asks and is allowed to drop her elbows so her bottom is in the air and she can rest her head on her hands.

We are there three hours and they sedate her before they let her out. We have more medication to give her tomorrow to keep her calm. I consider stealing a couple of tablets for myself for later, but I guess her need will be greater.

CHAPTER TWO

I lie in bed and listen to Graham's breathing. He is drugged up on the temazepam he had on repeat prescription last time he had sciatica. When I got to bed I shook the bottle, expecting it to rattle, but it was empty. He hadn't even thought to save some for me. His face is still and lifeless, all expression gone. I envy his ability to shut off and give himself over to unconsciousness, even if it is chemically induced. My shoulder blades ache. I try to relax them, make them drop, but the pain diverts to my neck. I shut my eyes and redness glows beyond my eyelids until purple dots swirl and merge into the shapes of faces. I dispel them and they disappear only to come back more grotesque every time until I come to the final face, ocean blue and bloated, eyes eaten out of their sockets, a nibbled gash for a mouth. The same face as last time. The same face as every time for the last twenty-five years.

When I can't sleep I mimic Graham's breathing, in with him and out with him. The hypnotic regularity of it is usually enough for me to drift off. Only it didn't work last night, I feel like I haven't slept a wink. Except I must have drifted off at some point because I dream I can hear waves lapping close by and the call of a blackbird. There's a meteorite shower and above it a haze of purple planets. It's magical but then my legs become entangled and I can't release them. I'm trapped and my head is cold. I hear a rattle and on the bed beside me I see a cockroach scuttling across the bottom sheet straight towards me. I can't move, I'm stuck. I wake frantically slapping my stomach to brush the cockroach away, only there's nothing there. Just Graham sleeping undisturbed.

I throw the duvet off and sit up. He shouts out in his sleep then mumbles and I place my hand on his shoulder. He is immediately silent and his breathing returns to normal. He could sleep on a washing line, even without the temazepam. My dressing gown is hanging on the back of the chair and I pick it up, still a little damp around the collar from where I washed my hair yesterday. I pull it around me hoping to get back some of the peace of mind from the day before, but it is impossible.

I peep in on Holly as I make my way downstairs. I creep down so as not to disturb my sleeping family. I need time alone to collect my thoughts. To make some sense of things; try to consider what should be done next. As if I have any control over anything, as if it isn't all just spiralling away from me. I pick up the Italian percolator from the glass shelf above the draining board and unscrew it but I can't be bothered. Instead I flick the kettle switch and spoon instant coffee into a mug. I open the kitchen drawer, bursting with junk and feel past the bits and bobs, rubber bands, dressmaker's tape, old eye drops, envelopes and an oversized box of Cook's matches and find the cigarettes I hide there. Nobody knows about them. My little secret. It does no harm; I can't smoke more than ten a week. My little crutch for when I need it. I take the matches too and open the back door, leaning on the door frame in the chill of the dawn air, taking down smoke deep into my lungs, light-headed from my nicotine hit.

It's raining gently and the garden is pitch-black; the hedges form a wall of dense blackness. The sky above is lightening in the east, trails of pink tendrils snake across the sky, harbingers of more bad weather. I don't step outside, I don't want to set off the security light, not yet, not until I've had these five minutes to myself. Yesterday we went to buy Holly a mosquito net for her trip to Nepal with the school as part of her Duke of Edinburgh award scheme. She didn't want one but Graham insisted. They had a huge fight about it. Life wasn't perfect but it was a damn sight better than it felt now. I finish my cigarette and dot it out on the ground. The garden lights come on as I cross the patio to throw the butt in the black landfill bin wondering if it should be recycled, wonder what difference a tiny fag-butt could make to global warming. I go to the downstairs bathroom and wash my hands and gargle with mouthwash to get rid of the smell of the cigarettes before anyone else gets up.

I nurse my coffee cup and sit quietly at the kitchen table fingering an appointment card they gave me at the hospital last night before we left with a number to call if we need anything. I put it out of my mind. I don't want strangers in the house again, asking questions, making value judgements on my family. Not yet. We need to cluster and regroup. We can deal with nurturing Holly for now.

She's upstairs now, wrapped in her fluffy white bathrobe, scrubbed clean, fast asleep. I bow my head and shiver. My baby girl, all grown up, but not grown up enough for this. At least I know it's not her first time. Last Christmas she had me trawling round North London before lunch looking for an emergency chemist to get her the morning after pill, so I know she's been active for some time.

I'm struck by the impropriety of my sentiment and wonder at the relevance of her sexual history. None to me but to the rest of the world I don't know, there's no manuals on how to deal with the rape of your teenage daughter. No dos and don'ts. No checklists to tick off before you allow your child out into the world on their own. I remember that day on the beach when she was little and she ran off. I was getting the picnic ready, preoccupied for a moment only. When I looked up Graham was out in deep water and Holly's bucket and spade lay beside me unattended. I ran to the water's edge when I realised she wasn't there, shouting to Graham to come back in. At first he thought I was just waving to him and he waved back. Later he said he noticed immediately that Holly wasn't there, but I don't believe him. If that were true, why wave back?

In the time it took for him to swim back to shore, I had created quite a scene. Other women swarmed round me, clasping their own children to them protectively, dispatching their husbands down the beach in search of a child they did not know. It was chaos. Graham and I ran in opposite directions along the shoreline calling her name. I was terrified; I remember thinking, if it has to be anything, please let it be the sea that has her. By the time I found a lifeguard I was frantic. He did his best to calm me. 'Kids go missing all the time, they always turn up, you'll see,' he said. I remember thinking that was true, except when it wasn't. It felt like someone had torn into my body and left just a gaping hole where my strength should be.

When I saw Graham running towards me with Holly in his arms, the relief was overwhelming. He'd found her looking in the shop at the top of the slipway where they sold trolls. She was obsessed with them. I grabbed her and I screamed at her. I remember it well. It was all I could do not to hit her I was so angry with her for going off. She stared at me blankly, like she had no idea what I was trying to say. The same blank expression she had when we arrived at the hospital with the police. I wipe away a tear with the heel of my hand. She was only gone for half an hour but I have replayed those moments over in my mind for more than a decade.

—

I hear the sound of someone moving around upstairs, the toilet flush and the soft padding of slippered feet on the thick carpet. A cough confirms what I already know; Holly's up. I stand and scrape the leg of the chair on the tiled floor.

'You all right? You want some help, love?' I call up the stairs.

'I'm not an invalid. I can make it down the stairs on my own,' comes Holly's reply.

Already, I've got it wrong. I need to back off. If she needs me she will let me know. I hear her haul herself down the stairs holding onto the bannister. She reaches the bottom of the stairs and her head is bowed as she carefully makes her way to the kitchen. She grasps the chair opposite me and gingerly sits down. She looks dreadful. Her eyes dull and bloodshot, deep within dark sockets and her skin grey. I don't know how to play it. I feel like I should try to be bright; I don't want her to think she is in trouble. But when she sits and looks at me I feel hollow and lost. I'm not sure how to help her so I reach out across the table and place her hands in mine.

'Are you OK, love?' I say. I always do this; ask if everything is OK when I know it isn't. She raises her eyes to look at me and I see the shadow of a bruise around her jawline.

'I'm sorry, Mum,' she says and drops her eyes again crying. I feel myself well up. The frustration is unbearable. My sense of failure as a parent is almost overwhelming. I get up and go round to her and put my arms around her shoulders drawing her to me. She winces and I relax my hold on her but keep her close enough that I can smell the apple shampoo in her hair and the faint residue of antiseptic from the hospital. 'What if I'm pregnant?' she asks.

'You won't be pregnant. They gave you the morning after pill. Remember?'

'They gave me lots of pills.'

She looks like a little girl again, trusting me to make it all better. It's the least of my worries, a pregnancy can be fixed. But what if she's caught something or she's been made infertile... I overheard the doctor last night tell the police her internal injuries seemed insubstantial but there was no way of knowing at this stage if there was any permanent damage. I want to ask her about her pain but it seems somehow inappropriate, like I'm prying into her private life. All she's said to me since it happened was she's sorry. I don't even know what she had said to the police. Or the counsellor, whoever the fuck it was. I don't know, everything was a blur. 'You want a coffee?' I ask. 'Or hot chocolate?'

She wants chocolate so I take out the milk pan. The electric whisk buzzes in my hand as I froth the milk, over-engineering the process, a tactic of avoidance to delay us having to broach the subject. I place the drink before her and touch her lightly on the shoulder.

'There you go, love. Drink up, it'll make you feel better.'

'Please don't offer to bake brownies,' she says. We both laugh. Upstairs we hear Graham getting out of bed.

'Tell me what happened,' I say. She places her elbow on the table and rubs the side of her face. She's thinking. 'Before he comes down. I'll back you, whatever. You know that.' I reach out open palmed across the table. 'It'll be easier if you just tell me first.'

'I got chucked out of Copa,' she says.

'Right.' She's not even old enough to go there but I can't pretend I don't know she does. I've even picked her up from there before now. We never tell Graham, he'd go mad. 'Why'd you go there?'

She blows on her chocolate and a hole appears in the froth at the top of her cup. She says, 'I heard Peter was going to be there.'

'Was he?'

'Yeah, with his new girlfriend from uni.' She tips her voice up into a sneer as she says 'uni.' Holly's been chasing after Peter all through Year Twelve and now he's at Durham reading Geology. He's quiet, I can't quite work out what Holly sees in him. Perhaps it's because he's never been particularly interested in her. She's not used to rejection. She's an only child, she doesn't take it easy when things don't go her way.

'Where was Sophie? I thought you two were together.' Holly and Sophie have been inseparable since Reception; they always go out together on Saturday night.

'She wouldn't leave the school disco. She's got really boring lately. All she talks about is her boyfriend and getting into Cardiff. And that Alice is always around. Just cos their boyfriends are best friends, doesn't mean they have to be.' Holly sniffs and wipes her nose on the back of her hand.

'So who were you with?'

'I met this girl from Hatfield, on her own.'

'Sounds like a popular girl,' I say.

'She knew everyone – all the footballers. That's how we got into the VIP area.'

'I bet.'

'What's that supposed to mean? You bet?'

'Just tell me what happened. I don't want to fight with you, Holly. I want to be supportive.'

'We met these blokes, they bought us champagne and sambuca shots. I refilled the glasses with that tequila you gave me, but we got caught and slung out.' She sips her chocolate and licks brown froth from her top lip. I want to tell her not to tell her dad but I stop myself.

'So, then what happened?'

'We went to the Premier Inn for a party.'

'What, at the Premier Inn?'

'In a room. Turned out there wasn't a party. It was just a rumour.'

'So why didn't you just come home then?'

'I didn't have the money for a cab.'

'You could have called me.'

She shrugs, 'I thought you were drinking.'

'I would still have come out. I've done it before.' It's true, I had been drinking wine but I would have been fine to drive. Perhaps not legally, but I would have gone out, it would have been fine. 'Anyway, didn't your dad set you up with an Uber account?'

'I forgot.' Holly sips at her chocolate nervously.

'Go on,' I encourage her.

'We dodged the security and found an empty room.'

I raise my eyebrow. 'Who did?'

'Me and the bloke I was with.'

'What bloke?'

'One of the footballers.'

'You didn't even know him, Holly. What were you thinking?'

'It wasn't him, Mum. He was lovely. Really gorgeous.'

'What happened then?'

'I was kissing him, that's all.'

'On the bed?'

'I guess.' She scrapes the froth from the edge of her cup with a teaspoon. 'He was really good looking.'

'Right.'

'We were getting off with each other, kissing and that. I've never done it before Mum, honest.'

'It?'

'You know, picked up a guy in a club.' Her shoulders tense and she sits back in her chair.

'OK,' I didn't know what to say. I know she wasn't a virgin, she slept with Peter last summer before he went away. But what she was describing wasn't like that, she was in love albeit unrequited. This is trawling a club and picking up a man for sex. So sordid. Rage thumped the blood through my ears. Sordid, but not rape, not as I understand it. I hear Graham cross the upstairs landing and lock the bathroom door. 'Go on,' I say.

'It was really dark. I couldn't see a thing but I heard the door open and someone came in. We'd just finished and I was lying back on the bed, getting my breath back. I thought I was hearing things. I remember shutting the door properly. I don't know who he was. He didn't speak to me.'

'What did he do?'

'He said it was his go.' She pauses and drops her gaze. 'So the lad I was with said he was done anyway and got up. Then this other guy sat on the bed. He pulled his trousers down to his knees. He didn't speak to me or anything. He didn't even take his shoes off.' Her voice is cracking up. She covers her mouth.

'What did you say? Did you tell him to stop?'

'Yes. I said I didn't want it. I tried to get up. But he was too strong. He held me down by my shoulders and, you know...' She pauses and takes a couple of deep breaths. She continues, 'When he finished, he got up and they left. The next thing I knew security were with me and then the police.' A single tear rolls down her cheek. I feel in my pocket for a tissue and offer it to her. She refuses it with a shake of her head and points at me so instead I dry my own face.

I'm crying more than she is. I'm not just crying for Holly, but for the girl all those years ago who had nobody to confide in. As hard as it is for me to hear, at least my daughter has a voice.

Laura Joyce
AFTERWORD

I have had the pleasure of working with the first cohort of students on the Crime Fiction MA at UEA from its inception in September 2015. I have been consistently surprised and delighted by their talent, innovation, ingenuity, and collegial spirit. The quality of the writing in this anthology reflects the progress that each of these crime authors has made over the course of the programme, not only in their own writing, but in immersing themselves in the crime genre. We have covered many subgenres, including noir, thrillers, domestic suspense, ritual murder, forensics, global bestsellers, true crime, and crime in translation. The students are now experts in police procedure, the criminal justice system, the laws on stalking, forensic analysis, and the rights of the dead, having taken a strongly interdisciplinary approach to their learning that extended beyond the reading of novels and essays into practical sessions with experts, interviews with practitioners, and trips to forensic facilities and the hospital mortuary. These students are researchers, essayists, critics, and practitioners as well as being outstanding authors. The writing in this anthology reflects their expertise and innovation as much as it does their commitment to craft. I have enjoyed working with them immensely, and know that each is a far stronger writer than when they began two years ago. Both the quality and variety of this anthology is testament to that.

May 2017

ACKNOWLEDGEMENTS

This anthology comprises excerpts from the novels written by the 2017 cohort in UEA's Creative Writing Master of Arts in Crime Fiction. The anthology would not have been possible without the generosity of the UEA School of Literature, Drama and Creative Writing in partnership with Egg Box Publishing.

We would like to thank our tutors Tom Benn, Laura Joyce, and programme director Henry Sutton for their guidance and inspiration. Behind the scenes, Laura Leech has been indispensable. Andrew Cowan, co-director of the Creative Writing Programme, and Philip Langeskov offered their support.

Guest lecturers have been a highlight of the programme. We would like to offer our special thanks to novelists Mark Billingham, Lee Child, Julia Crouch, Melanie McGrath, Ian Rankin, and Denise Mina for their fascinating masterclasses, and crime and forensic experts Dr Stephen Day, Ian Sales, and Dr Mark Wilkinson for their riveting seminars.

Our editorial team included UEA Publishing Project's Nathan Hamilton, managing editor Rachel Hore, copy editor Andrew Turner, and editors Suzanne Mustacich and Trevor Wood, with a Herculean contribution from editor Harriet Tyce.

UEA Creative Writing MA Anthology: Crime writing, 2017

First published by Egg Box Publishing, 2017
part of UEA Publishing Project Ltd.

A CIP record for this book is available from the British Library.
Printed and bound in the UK by Imprint Digital.

Designed by Emily Benton.
emilybentonbookdesigner.co.uk

Proofread by Sarah Gooderson.
Distributed by NBN International
10 Thornbury Road Plymouth
PL6 7PPT +44 (0)1752 2023102
e.cservs@nbninternational.com

ISBN: 978-1-911343-26-4